THE A
HORRIBLE
PEOPLE

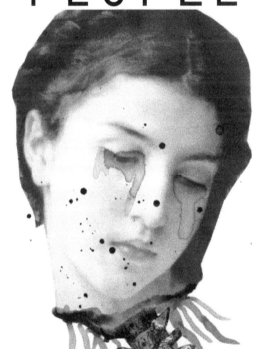

JOHN
SKIPP

LAZY FASCIST PRESS
P.O. BOX 10065
PORTLAND, OR 97296

ISBN: 978-1-62105-193-0

Copyright © 2015 by John Skipp

Cover Design by Matthew Revert

Interior Design by Cameron Pierce

Printed in the USA.

CONTENTS

THE TWO JOHNS OR FAKE GUM:

AN INTRODUCTION BY JOSH MALERMAN

Let's have fun. Yes? Let's have fun.

Two artists are putting on a show. One of them is a tortured, brooding, dark artist who stands before a closed curtain, ready to pull the thing back.

"And *now!*" he bellows, eyes ablaze. "I will reveal… *the truth!*"

The audience is expecting something atrocious; a beast that really represents man, embarrasses him even.

The first artist pulls the curtain back.

Revealing, of course, the second.

But this guy… he's jovial, joyful, riding a tricycle, dinging the bell. The only person scared of *this* guy is the first artist who so wanted to expose the dark shit, the pain, the rot.

But what can he do? What can anybody do but marvel at the second artist for his fluidity while applauding the first for his reveal?

"Genius is torture!" the first scowls, offstage but within earshot.

"Torture?" says the second, cross-eyed and giggling. "There's nothing to it!"

Meet John Skipp. In *The Art of Horrible People* he plays both roles. The man with something really nasty to show us, and the man who honks the clown horn after we've seen it. He'll introduce himself as a monster, then shake your hand with a buzzer. It's not an easy thing to do, and probably a much more delicate thing to *be*.

Horrible People smacks of autobiographical run-ins; John lives in Los Angeles and encounters more than his share of crud. But he hasn't gotten cynical. Hasn't gotten mean. Would you? You might. People do. John, instead, has dropped a lot of that stuff into his tri-colored story-machine; in goes the bullshit… and out comes…

The *fun*.

Take "Skipp's Hollywood Alphabet Soup of Horror." If this isn't the centerpiece of the collection (let's give that distinction to "Food Fight"), then it's sure as hell the blueprint.

E IS FOR EGO: If I can picture it, it is already mine.

John guides us through the whole alphabet, describing Hollywood in a way we've never read before. Sometimes it's funny, but mostly it makes your stomach hurt, worrying about the people who go to LA with a mind to "make it" rather than using the imagination it takes to "make it up."

Let's flip back to our two artists, the two Johns. The first,

2

the truth seeker, he's offstage, shaking his head, saying, "Ah! Los Angeles is in ruins!"

The second turns to him, smiling, "Great! Let's juggle it!"

John's juggling LA here. And we could watch him do it all night.

I'm thinking about the first story in this collection, "Art is the Devil." I'm thinking about the exchange between Vale and Kristy, discussing Max Apocalypso:

"*He's not really a douche,*" (Vale) said. "*He's just run out of patience with facile Hollywood dogshit.*"

"*Fair enough,*" Kristy said. "*So what's his great vision?*"

John's Max Apocalypso *does* have a vision. A devastating one at that.

Is it good?

Ah, the art of horrible people...

It's Los Angeles gone mad, and the book only gets madder as the stories roll out. The unsane exhibitions in "Art is the Devil" become downright depressing in "Depresso the Clown." But can you blame the girl? Do you respect her for facing her fears?

You might.

Horrible people?

Maybe.

And who's more horrible than the monsters who attack when "Rose Goes Shopping"? Now we've got a battle. And in a battle there's *death*. And in death there are worms. And the titular characters in "Worm Central Tonite!" gotta eat, too.

Horrible People lifts, higher... all the way to the "Soup of Horror," where an entire second movement is born. John has lead us, almost musically, to the plateau, where the meat is. "Zygote Notes on the Imminent Birth of a Feature Film as Yet Unformed," "In the Waiting Room, Trading Death Stories," and "Food Fight" are a trio as magnificent as any you've read anyplace else.

"Bravo!" says our second artist, sawing himself in half on stage now, belly-laughing away. "A crescendo!"

"But there's so much suffering in there," the first artist counters. "What about the softball team?"

"Don't you get it by now?" the second artist says. "It's *your* job to bring out the terrible, and *mine* to play with it."

John sure as hell plays with his food in "Food Fight," an instant movie that's gotta be made. An absolute stunner that begins *BLAMMO!* at the peak of the madness, the revolt, the humor and suffering, everything that John has built up through the seven stories before it.

"I see it now!" says our first artist, rising at last, feeling less burdened by observation.

"What do you see?" says our second, sitting on a whoopee cushion as big as a couch.

"Art is *beyond* horrible people. Beyond horrible or honorable, noble or needy."

"Yes!" cries the second, still playing, always playing with the observations of the first. "But what is *art?*"

Of course there aren't two artists behind *The Art of Horrible People.* There is only John Skipp. And though he's famous for collaborating, here we got lucky. Because this time John collaborated with himself. The two Johns. The one who pulls back the curtain and gives us the truth… and the one who hands it fake gum.

Savor this book. Savor this writer.

And savor some fake gum, for truth's sake.

THE ART OF
HORRIBLE
PEOPLE

ART IS THE DEVIL

It was Charlie Sheen night at the Hyaena Art Gallery. One actor's implosion was every other man's meat. And Kristy had to admit she wished she'd been in on it, despite her automatic sell-out reservations.

This was one hilarious, legitimately badass show. In retrospect, she was kicking herself for not having even tried.

Art was *supposed* to be provocative and fun. Otherwise, what was the fucking point? Excite the eye, and you excite the soul. Everything else was pretense.

These super-cool artists had brought it: all the absurdity and pathos, indictment and entitlement, sincere mockery and star-loving devotion that such pop culture work demanded. Hyaena had set the bar high, in the lowest way possible. And that was a beautiful thing.

"I like the one where he's flying in his underwear, drinking coffee and shitting missiles that blow up the world," Drea said, lighting her cigarette on the sidewalk outside, less than twenty feet from the door, in flagrant violation of Burbank law.

Across the street was the distinctive neon sign of the Safari Hotel, where James Gandolfini menaced Patricia Arquette in *True Romance*, one of Drea's favorite all-time films. They'd already spent twenty minutes discussing how cool that was. How *insanely* cool it was to be in the place where shit actually happens.

So far from South Dakota, where carving dead presidents' heads into mountains was the state's last great artistic achievement. The place from which they'd escaped, heading west to Los Angeles, in the prime of their lives. To take their own shots at greatness.

"I really liked Charlie as Alladin Sane," Kristy said. "And not just for the Bowie reference."

"The one with the huge cock and machete was gorgeous."

Kristy laughed. "And the demonically-possessed one was soooooo realistic."

"I bet he's a really fun guy to hang out with, if you're not a hot woman."

"Which pretty much rules you out."

"Rules *both* of us out, baby," Drea said, flashing her best friend a wink. "Charlie Sheen would fuck you in a second."

"Yeesh."

"Just sayin'."

Traffic was slow on Olive Ave. at 10:30 on a Friday night. Most of the standing-room-only crowd had dispersed an hour ago, once the media frenzy had been sated.

So when the clankity black 1962 Cadillac hearse pulled up out front, they were the two eye-candiest women on the pavement.

Kristy, pale and lovely, a lithe redheaded sprite in a bright green summer frock. Drea, bursting out in voluptuous dark starlet splendor, like young Jennifer Connelly in a blood-red contour-clinging dress.

Together, they looked like the world's best Christmas present.

The shotgun window of the hearse rolled down, and a bald creepy man's face poked out through the gap, sporting thick black eyeliner and matching pointed goatee.

"Look at you," he said, appraising them both. "Out here, wasting your time."

"I'm enjoying my time very much, thank you," Drea said. "What the fuck do you care?"

The bald man snickered. That was the only word for it. "You think this art is transgressive?"

"It's fun," Drea said.

"It's really good," Kristy added, cheerfully defensive.

"Sure. For lightweights. Have you ever *seen* real art?"

"My friend makes real art," Drea said, pointing with her cigarette, free hand balling into a fist. Always a red flag with Drea.

He cast Kristy a dismissive glance. "Yes, I'm sure her Ken doll with the word 'Winning' writ large in Elmer's glue and glitter was a big hit with the crowd."

Kristy bristled under his black-eyed gaze. Her Barbie-art diorama phase in junior high was kind of embarrassing, yes; but she'd learned a lot from it. And fuck him for pegging her there.

"Excuse me, you dime store Satanist prick," Drea said, and it was his turn to bristle. "If this show is so stupid and shitty, then why are you here?"

"I think you're jealous," Kristy said.

"Of *this?*" He let out a mad scientist laugh from the Vincent Price School of Cartoon Villainy. "Oh, please."

"No, really," Kristy persisted. "What, so you're a 'real' artist? Where's the line to get into *your* show?"

"And why are you rattling around in that clunker?" added Drea. "Trolling other people's parties on a Friday night?"

It was fun to watch his ego try to contain itself. It was so clear that he wanted to explode like one of Charlie Sheen's ass-bombs.

Hollywood egos were like that, they'd found. Intensely superficial, fronting all the time, with a whole lot of unresolved damage underneath.

Kristy and Drea knew all about unresolved damage. They had just decided to not let it turn them into assholes. Made a pact to hang onto their souls. Keep their feet on the ground.

And always, always back each other up.

From the driver's seat of the hearse, two pale sleek elegant feminine hands reached out to firmly massage his shoulders. He groaned, eyes rolled back, then centered himself.

"Thank you, Vale," he said, and the hands withdrew. "You always know just what to do."

Kristy and Drea threw grinning *what the fuck* looks at each other, turned back to Little Baldy, eager to see what happened next.

"My new show," he said, with a great mustered air of dignity, "is about to debut."

"How exciting for you," Drea said.

"But we're throwing a little pre-launch party tonight,"

he continued. "A midnight premiere."

"Well, have a nice time…" Kristy said, turning away.

The driver's door opened.

And the driver emerged.

"Omigod," Drea said. And something in the way she said it told Kristy she might want to turn back around and see.

The woman driving the hearse was unearthly in her beauty, an easily six-foot Bettie Page, white angel face framed by black devil hair, the bangs straight across the fierce penciled-in eyebrows and bright blue shining eyes. Her nose, cheeks, lips and chin were so perfect in symmetry that she almost had to be sculpted by the finest porn star plastic surgery techniques.

As she rounded the front of the hearse, runway-walking toward them, her body in motion was almost not to be believed. The girls were both gym fanatics, and roughly as taut as could be; but this woman looked like a superhero drawing, a fanboy jackoff hallucination of what femininity ought to be.

Or fangirl jackoff, for that matter.

Drea was not gay—she had guy-cravings, too—but when it came to otherworldly Amazon women like this, the part of her brain that was 100% dude went into total sexual how-can-I-nail-this overdrive.

Kristy could clearly see her friend fighting back the drool. Wiped the corners of her own mouth, just in case. Took a drag off her smoke. And stepped forward, to Drea's side.

She'd almost completely forgotten about the creepy guy, watching, until the woman's too-perfect breasts were obscured by a pair of postcard-sized invitations.

And then the woman named Vale was upon them.

"He's a genius," the driver said, looking them each in the eye. "And believe me, I know genius when I see it. You should totally come."

"Um," Kristy said, taking the invitation in her hand. The words ART IS THE DEVIL briefly distracted her from staring.

"Fuck Charlie Sheen," Vale continued. "That's the shallow end of the pool. This town is crawling with dead ends, false hopes, and empty promises, right?"

"Well, yeah…" Drea said.

"So when you find something real, that cuts through the bullshit, and speaks to the highest, smartest part of yourself, you want to fight for that vision."

"Well, sure," Drea said. "But…"

Kristy finished the question.

"Why's your guy such a douche?"

It was a moment of truth, and Kristy half-expected a slap in the face. But instead of getting defensive, Vale just laughed, as if delighted by the challenge.

"He's not really a douche," she said. "He's just run out of patience with facile Hollywood dogshit. He's so sensitive, and his work goes so much deeper, that it kills him when otherwise intelligent people make do with lowest-common-denominator tripe. Never knowing how much better it gets."

"Fair enough," Kristy said. "So what's his great vision?"

Vale brought her index finger to her own lush red lips, as if to say *shhh*. Kissed the finger. Then reached out to dab that lipstick kiss on the tip of Kristy's nose.

"Boop," she said. "Only one way to find out."

And with that, Vale turned and went back to the Caddy, leaving the girls to watch her stunning ass in something like shock.

While the creepy genius lit a black cigarette, let the smoke plume out slowly in unreadable thought balloons.

***

Five minutes later, Drea was behind the wheel, hopping the Olive entrance onto the I-5 South, heading downtown.

"Fuck *yeah*, I wanna see his stupid show!" She was ranting, stomping down hard on the gas, pushing her leased Prius from 20 to 80 in the time it took to merge. "He better be fucking transcendent, is all I gotta say."

"*Remain on the 5 for another 6.5 miles,*" said her dashboard GPS.

"I found his website," Kristy crowed from the passenger seat, diddling her iPhone. "Max Apocalypso. Right there. You can't say he's not subtle."

"Max Pretensalypso." Kicking her speed up to 90.

"I was thinking more Missed Testocalypso."

"Or Baron Von Blowme."

Kristy laughed. "I bet he wears sneakers with IHEARTSATAN666 scrawled across them in magic marker… ooo. Ooo. Wait."

"What? You find some 'real art?'" She sniggered.

"No." Kristy was transfixed by her screen. "Or yes. But none of it's his."

"What, he's a plagiarist? HA! That fuck!"

"No. It says…" Scrolling. "It says he's pulled all of his art off the internet. That's why all the Giger and Bosch.

And here's a direct quote: 'The enormity of my work is such that it can only be experienced firsthand. These are installation pieces of epic scale. To move inside them is to truly immerse yourself in…'—I'm sorry, this is funny—'…in the intimate gnosis of neverending Hell. Soon, all of you will know its glory.'"

Drea laughed. "Sounds like truth in advertising to me. Except for, you know, the part about anyone knowing."

"Yeah." Kristy got thoughtful. "But the thing is, I kind of get what he means. Like, pictures of the monsters and props at a really good haunted Halloween Spook House are not nearly as cool as walking through the Spook House itself. And you *don't* wanna give away all the scares and surprises. That takes half the fun out of it."

"Yeah…"

"So maybe he's not a total douche," Kristy continued, speculatively playing the thread out. "Maybe that's just part of his act. Trying to see how many people he can get to hate him."

"Well," Drea said, "he's off to an excellent start."

"Maybe Elvira was right, and he's just a misunderstood genius. Maybe he's got a thing about show biz. Like, maybe his daddy's a huge movie star who used to bang his little ass whenever the starlets ran out."

"Yeah. Wow. Could be." Drea snorted, contemptuous. "Why are you trying to rationalize his behavior, all of a sudden?"

"I don't know." Kristy laughed. "Maybe I'm trying to justify wasting our time, checking out his pompous crap."

"*Exit I-5 in one mile,*" said the GPS, as Drea impulsively pushed it to 100.

***

It took another ten minutes to negotiate the downtown Los Angeles labyrinth, follow the robot voice to that one faceless gray industrial monolith out of a trillion.

But they found it. Or at least found the address on the postcard: entrance lights on, no one standing outside. It was a desolate building on a grim empty stretch, and there was plenty of parking out front, which led them to suspect that maybe poor ol' Max E. Pad wasn't getting the sophisticated turnout he'd hoped for.

His hearse was right there, though, in the gated lot to the left. So there was no mistaking that this was the place.

"Okay," Kristy said. "Are we sure we wanna do this?"

"Well, we're here," Drea said, pulling up to the curb.

"What if she's not even there? Like, she was an actress he just hired to drive him around, try to lure in pussy?"

"If he could afford to hire a woman like that, and get her to testify that hard on his behalf, without breaking character, then he could probably afford to fuck her. At which point, what does he need *us* for?"

Drea left the engine running as they thought about that.

"You think she's really fucking him?" Kristy asked.

"I hate to even consider it."

"I know."

"That said, I've never seen so many ugly men nailing beautiful women as I have in Hollywood. So he must have money."

"These lofts aren't cheap."

"So let's say she's an actress, and she's part of his show…"

"The only good part, so far."

"What if this is some Satanist cult thing, and he's just trying to recruit us?"

Drea cackled. "Then he's shit out of luck."

"Are you packing tonight?"

"Are you kidding?"

"Me, too."

"Okay, then." They high-fived, hugged each other with their seat belts still on, which was kind of hilarious.

Then unfastened themselves, and got out of the car.

***

Kristy waved hi to the security cam as Drea rang the bell. The response was almost instantaneous. Buzz, click, and they were in.

The stark foyer was lit in cold blue, punctured by irregular, shifting stabs of glaring white and strobing red. The walls were painted in high-gloss black, reflecting the light while seeming to disappear behind it, so that the veneer pulsed at a low hum with nothing but nothingness beyond, creating a 30 foot square box inside infinity.

"That's a cool effect," Kristy said.

As the door slammed shut behind them.

At the far end of the room was a glowing doorway, lined in Kubrickian blinding white. A dark silhouette stood neatly at its center, facing them, the white and red lights landing everywhere but there.

Above it was a neon sign that said:

DEATH WILL BE YOUR GUIDE

"Very artistical," Drea said.

"Shhh…"

As they advanced toward their shadow guide, their own footsteps echoed back at them from hidden speakers throughout the room. It was a slick Sensurround trick, made it feel like invisible others were approaching from behind, ahead, to either side. They found themselves glancing nervously over their shoulders, saw nothing.

"They must have directional mics at floor level," Drea said. "That's smart."

"This is creepy."

"Yeah. Shit!" Getting into the spookhouse thrill.

Ten feet from the glowing doorway, Death's silhouette began to back into the corridor behind it, still facing them. For the first time, they could clearly see the black robe and hood that entirely concealed it.

Could see the Steadicam rig attached to its torso, straps also black. And the high-end hi-def camera aimed straight at their faces, with what looked like a very wide lens.

"Oh, really?" Drea said, this time straight to the camera. "If you wanna use this footage, we're gonna have to sign release forms, okay? I'm SAG eligible! I get paid for this shit!"

"Not to ruin your shot or anything!" Kristy added helpfully.

"They try to rope me into working for free, his new name's gonna be Max I-Punch-Your-Dick, Yo."

"I think they got the message. You wanna look scared for a second, just to be nice?"

"Fuck that." Drea flipped the double bird. "You want my cooperation? You gotta earn my respect. And be nice to my friend."

Kristy knew better than to argue. Not being an actress, she put on her best "I'm really scared" face for the camera, then giggled, embarrassed.

As they entered the doorway of light, it suddenly surged to a painful intensity. They yelped, blinded, blocked their eyes with their hands.

And passed over to the other side.

***

Blinking and cursing, the first thing Kristy noticed was the sound: a low, near-subsonic *whoom* that rattled her fillings.

"DAMN it!" she yelled, could barely hear her own voice.

Then she saw Drea, three feet ahead, sticking fingers in her ears and laughing. *"Are you SEEING this shit?"* she hollered, as a thudding human heartbeat pummeled their guts from hidden speakers.

The corridor splayed out before them had been designed to resemble a 40-foot long walk-through uterus, walls and ceiling organically curved and glistening with gel. The whole thing was sculpted out of foam latex—an insane amount of it, maybe $20,000 worth—with little veins and moles and pulsing polyps running all the way through.

And prosthetic human arms, jutting out from either side. Dangling or groping from the walls, as if entrapped behind them. Total monster movie shit.

Some were cut off at the wrist. A few of them twitched. It had a *Hellraiser* vibe; a movie they both loved. And not cheaply done, either. This guy clearly had a budget.

"COME ON!" Drea roared.

"OKAY!"

"LET'S SEE WHAT ELSE THEY GOT! I BET THE STUPID HEAVY METAL STARTS UP ANY MINUTE!"

They pushed forward through the haunted canal together in single file, just out of reach of the grasping fingers, footsteps utterly drowned out by the sound. Kristy sped up enough to take her friend's hand, feeling stupid about how skeeved-out this was starting to make her.

From above, unevenly spaced lights went from bright to dim in sequence. And fog machines spritzed just enough to clarify the beams, amp every shadowed motion.

Thirty feet in, the light turned red above their heads. The flesh of the walls and ceilings sickened, went dark and greasy, began to sag and ooze and drip.

While the arms went from animatronic foam latex to something cruder, shrink-wrapped and glistening, bony and rotten to the eye.

That was when the bad smell kicked in.

Kristy and Drea had met in 8th grade biology class. Formaldehyde and frog—that baby pig they'd co-dissected—preceded weed, douche, cheap perfume, and burning Barbie hair in their earliest shared memories.

It was coming from one of the arms, where the shrink-wrap had torn. They both saw it at once.

There were dead maggots in the hole.

"We gotta go," Kristy choked.

And turned around.

Too late.

***

The first cloaked figure through the doorway of light was

easily seven feet tall. Even from thirty-five feet back, Drea could see its hooded head nearly scrape the ceiling, rapidly advancing toward them.

The next one was even larger.

And both of them had large curved blades—less machetes than scimitars—that glistened in the light. They did not look like props.

If this was a joke, it wasn't funny. She let go of Kristy's hand, dug into her purse.

Kristy was screaming, and that was okay. *Let it out, baby,* she thought. Fighting her own panic. Fingers closing on the object she sought.

Flicking off the safety before it even came out of the bag.

She couldn't shoot around her friend, so she whirled and took out the Steadicam Operator of Death with one shot to the body and another to the head. The robed figure fell backwards, spraying, inches from the curtain at the end of the hall.

The camera, she hoped, was undamaged. They would probably want that for evidence, later.

"COME ON!" she bellowed, turning back to make sure. Got a whiff of the pepper spray Kristy was unleashing, and started sprinting as fast as she could in the opposite direction.

Pushing deeper into Hell.

***

Kristy didn't carry a gun—didn't like them, was uncomfortable with them—but right now, she wished she had an AK handy to mow those fuckers down.

As it was, these closed quarters would put a serious hurt on their asses, the closer they got to the fog of pain she'd just laid down behind her.

She took off after Drea, her own eyes slightly burning, saw the curtains ahead and the dead body she would have to vault. Saw Drea, in control. Could hear the gunshots, slightly louder than the shrieks from behind her, all overwhelmed by the heartbeat from the speakers.

From which, God help them, heavy metal now emerged.

***

Drea wasn't about to run through anything her bullets hadn't softened up first. So she fired through the curtain, going left to right in a salvo, squeezing an extra one off to either side, then two more straight down the middle.

Please be dead, she prayed. *Whoever's out there, please be dead as of now.*

And the good news was—as she passed through the curtain—that there were two very surprised-looking black-robed motherfuckers on the floor before her, bleeding. Only one of them still moving. And not very well.

The bad news was the one she missed.

Who gutted her, three steps in.

***

And this is what Kristy saw, as she passed through the curtain, less than five seconds later.

Vale's beautiful face.

Drea, sagging from behind.

There was a scimitar sticking out of Drea's back. Then there wasn't. Drea buckled, no longer held up, gun firing at nothing as she dropped to her knees.

In the time it took Kristy to scream, the sneering Amazon kicked her dying friend out of the way, grabbed Kristy by the hair, and yanked her painfully forward.

"This is real art," the woman hissed in her ear, wrapping around her from behind, bringing the wet blade to her throat.

As all earthly Hell splayed out before her.

Max Apocalypso style.

***

The installation's nightmare *piece de resistance* had been constructed at a 45-degree angle: a long, sharp ramp upward that filled the width of the warehouse, entirely gobbling Kristy's view.

The centerpiece was an enormous five-pointed star— massively spotlit from above—rendered entirely in dozens of meat-packed mannequins, laid out foot to head, at least fifty feet in diameter. Their cracked plastic exteriors swarmed with flies, visible even at a distance.

The circle that encased them was most certainly drawn in blood.

The center of the Sigil—Satan's special pentagram—held a Warhol-like print of Max Apocalypso's face: glowering, ten feet tall. Just to clarify that it was all about him.

And filling the space outside of this frame were dozens of bodies—most of them dead, the rest emaciated and squirming—crucified upside-down, like fighter planes about to crash, metal spikes driven into their hands, bellies, and feet.

Above it all, in neon letters also ten feet high:

ART IS THE DEVIL!

WELCOME, SATAN!

Then the faithful filed in from either side, chanting indecipherably along with the death metal dirge. Maybe twenty in all. Most in robes. A few in jeans and t-shirts, probably crew, weirdly twice as scary for their absolute normalcy. Like this was just another non-union gig, with some psycho-killing afterlife points thrown in.

Finally, the Master of Ceremonies stepped before her, resplendent in robes that cost ten times as much as the net worth of her whole family tree put together, with an unctuous grin that was too much to bear.

"LORD SATAN...!" he began.

Kristy took it all in. Assessed her odds. Wished there were only some way to take them all down with her. Wished she could somehow tell Drea how incredibly sorry she was.

Then emptied the pepper spray over her shoulder.

As her throat sawed open, and her vision went gray.

***

"GAHHH!" Vale screamed, face and lungs on chemical fire. She let go of the fire-hosing red-headed chippie she'd just murdered and dropped to her own knees, blind and vomiting. They hit the floor in pluming unison, everyone else pulling back from the fumes and the spray.

"Where's my fucking Steadicam?" Max roared.

"Barry's dead!"

"Jesus FUCK! Can't you people do ANYTHING?"

"SORRY, MASTER!" several bellowed as one, scurrying to retrieve the rig or somehow make this right.

Max stood at the center of the chaos he'd created, desperately tried to figure out how to pull a save. He was surrounded by halfwits, his buzz utterly blown, along with the rest of his inheritance.

He'd thrown the last half-mil of his piece-of-shit sitcom-producing daddy's trust fund money into prepping this event. Had spent years cultivating this invocation—this ultimate expression—in his head. Hired dozens of artists to help realize his vision. Disappeared the ones that failed. Fitting their bodies—or pieces thereof—into the greater work.

The Empty Waiting Womb of Life and *The Grasping Passage to Perdition* were mere pre-game warm-ups. Important pieces, in their own right. But nothing but foreplay, to Max's way of seeing.

This was the one all Hell was waiting for. His ticket to its inner circle.

And there was Vale, puking and screaming on the floor. No help at all. So much for his right hand.

"Lord Satan…!" he repeated, and Vale screamed again, worse, rolling onto her back before the two dead girls and the pathway back.

The pathway burst into flames, as did all the walls surrounding them.

And Vale's perfect belly stretched, expanded, *ballooned*, in far-from-immaculate conception.

Max recoiled at the sight, as the temperature spiked, a super-heated 100-degree salvo that squeezed the sweat from his pores before he even knew what hit him. His pivoting gaze swept across the Sigil writ large. His own face at the center, suddenly melting and morphing.

The mannequins, beginning to stir.

Vale's next scream did not seem to even come from this earth, and Max reeled back just in time to watch her super-impregnated belly blow open like an all-meat Jiffy-Pop tray.

And two taloned hands shredded up through the hole.

Satan, rising.

All the way up from Hell.

***

The Devil wore a splendid black tux for the occasion, though his flesh was the exact color of the blood and gore that caked him as he snapped Vale's spine and ascended through the hole. It was as if there was a mechanized platform rising beneath him in an elaborate Broadway show, bringing him up to stage level.

A big entrance, after all, was the mark of a pro.

Vale's intestines were draped over his shoulders like garlands. He took a bite, just for shits and giggles, then tossed them off in a casually grandiloquent gesture that left his arms extended wide, as if to the welcome the applause.

Of course, everybody still alive was screaming in terror. He took that as a standing ovation.

As the rest wavered, paralyzed by fear, he stared straight at the host of the party, who had dropped to his knees in whimpering worship.

Satan took a hankie from his upper breast pocket, wiped away the spatter, arranged his dark bangs just so.

Revealing his true face, at last.

He looked a lot like Charlie Sheen.

***

"NOOOOO!!!" Max screamed, as if his soul would burst. But even that was not the worst.

"Dude?" the Prince of Darkness said, head cocked in jaunty contempt as he stepped out of Vale's still-screaming carcass and strode forward, cupping Max's chin with one massive palm, forcing Max's tear-filled eyes to rise and meet his fiery gaze.

"I hate to break this to you, but... that was the most pretentious piece of shit I've ever seen."

Max started to scream again, but the Sheen-faced Satan squeezed his windpipe shut, throttling it down to a peep, and leaned in close.

"Shhhh," he hissed, breath like pussy and sulfur. *"You had your chance. Now let me show you how it's done."*

The Devil snapped his fingers, and the death metal stopped. In its place, a blistering flurry of dissonant horns raked the air, with salvos of polyrhythmic drum and bass underneath.

With that, Satan's Big Band materialized behind him—a ten-piece, brass-led orchestra of the damned, framed by flames—and launched into a blistering funked-out 7/4 jazz groove. All playing at cranked-up virtuosity pitch, like the crazy-ass demons they were.

"Lesson #1," Satan said. *"WHERE'S THE FUN? Where's the zazz? Are you kidding me, Ace? Don't you even know what a fucking party is?"*

Max tried to answer, but his eyes and tongue were bugging out of his skull.

"What you built was like a meat locker still-life. So static. So pompous and stagy. So full of itself. It's embarrassing to think that's how little you know me, for all your so-called 'devotion'".

Satan Sheen painfully twisted Max's face back toward his diorama, which was now anything but static. The mannequins all crawling en masse down the ramp.

The dead, awakening, and tearing themselves free.

It was at this point that the crew began to panic, try to figure out how to escape. Turning this way and that, it was almost like dancing, inside an infinite circle of flame.

"Lesson #2, and this one is important," Satan said, loud enough to be heard above the saxophones and screaming. *"Never kill people who are cooler than you are.*

"Because that always just pisses me off."

***

Kristy and Drea woke up on the floor together. Each in their own pool of gore. They were dead, and then they weren't; but the first thing they did was turn to check on each other.

Kristy saw the band behind Drea—the hot horned trumpet player who was wailing his balls off, the couple of cloaked crusaders bursting into flames behind them—then focused back on her blood-drooling friend, who grinned as she rose up off the floor.

Drea was drawn to the undead hordes pouring off of that 45-degree angle and diving straight into Max's lackeys.

Limbs were being torn loose and strewn.

"LET'S GET IN ON THIS SHIT!" Drea howled.

"WOOOOOOO!!!"

Locking coal-red eyes and sharp-toothed grins, they leapt into the mayhem.

And lo and behold, just a couple feet away, the closest still-warm body was Vale: the official poster girl for talking the talk, then walking them straight to the slaughter. It was amazing that the chick was neither dead nor demonized: in a halfway place of inescapable total pain, rent asunder at the midriff.

"Let's see what you look like without that face," Drea said, brought her fresh claws to the task.

"Looks like an ugly skull that won't stop screaming," Kristy noted, squeezing Vale's fake boobs till the saline geysered. "WHEEE!!!"

All around them, people were dying, and that was utterly fantastic. Fuck these people. They completely deserved it. Kristy's dying wish was being granted one severed head at a time, one desiccate corpse in a victory dance, one mannequin swarm stripping the key grip down to his essential skeletal frame.

And then there was good ol' Max himself: choking and weeping on his knees, like the little bald bitch he was, as his Epic Work was undone before him. But he'd finally delivered on that whole 'intimate gnosis of neverending Hell' thing. At least he sure *looked* like he was in Hell.

The devil girls couldn't see who was pinning him there till the tall, handsome man turned to face them and beamed.

"Ladies…" he said, as they both shrieked with glee. And before they could state the obvious, added, *"Yeah, yeah. I*

like to tell Charlie that he looks just like me."

"OMIGOD!" Drea said. "Did you see the show at Hyaena tonight?"

Satan chuckled. *"I did. It was hilarious."*

"Wasn't it great?" Kristy gushed.

"Way better than this one, I'll tell you that!"

"WOOOOOO!!!" whooped the devil girls, delirious, as the last standing twig in Max's broken soul went snap.

"I'm kinda liking the afterparty, though. You want to thank your host personally?"

"Ohhhhh, please," Drea moaned. "We would like that very much."

"Is there any part of him," Kristy asked, "that you'd prefer we *not* thank?"

"Leave the eyes in the head, if you could," Satan said. *"So you'll always know that he's still watching."*

"Oooo," Drea cooed.

"He's gonna be stuck like that forever, after all. We wouldn't want him to miss a goddam thing."

"We promise," Kristy said, as the meat-drenched mannequins crawled up close to bear witness, surrounded by the dozens of leering corpses Max had made. Satan's jazz band propelled them, dialed the music in tight, made even the flames and shadows dance.

It was, she saw, a moment of staggering perfection.

"This is real art," Kristy informed Max, looking him dead in the eyes, then bloodily carving one word across his forehead with one razor-tipped index finger.

The word, of course, was *WINNING!*

And everybody laughed but him.

Depresso the Clown

It's a rancid corn dog breakfast again. She slides it under the door, on the unwashed plastic tray. The note on the tray says GOOD MORNING, FREAK! Otherwise, I'd have no way of knowing.

There are no windows in this basement. No light but the jittering fluorescents overhead. Forever on. Forever just out of reach. Like the door. The walls. The many sharp and painful objects.

All the other things they've kept hidden from the world.

I awake on the cold concrete, face as far from the drain as the chains will allow. And my face is ablaze with smoldering pain, like a million tiny insect stings. I swat at it with my padded hands, but that only makes it worse.

I try to say something, but I no longer can.

I hear her laugh, as she heads back up the stairs. And that sound, more than anything, brings the burning tears again. There is no surgery short of death that can keep my soul from sobbing.

"Aw, poor baby," she says. "Now THAT'S funny!"

Then I'm alone with my sorrow, my corn dog, and pain.

***

I wish I could remember the date exactly. The twenty-somethingth of August of this year. It was hot, I can tell you that. So hot my makeup was running. I was on break between shows, catching a quick smoke out back, when this guy came walking up and said, "Hey."

"Hey," I said back, not really looking, scoping out the less-than-half-empty parking lot. Not a whole lot of people that day. Business had been in the crapper for years, was not getting any better.

"You get high?" he said, and that got my attention. I'd been nursing my last gram of Sour Cheese Diesel for over a week. Rob kept saying he'd score for sure in the next town, but it just kept not happening. And we were days out from medico-legal Michigan.

"You're talkin' weed, right?" I said.

"I'm talkin' whatever you want." He grinned, showing godawful teeth. He had the scrawny scarecrow look of a third-string high school basketball player who found crack and then woke up ten years later, still wearing the same t-shirt.

Any fear that he might be an undercover cop vanished right there. Just another local loser, working us like we worked them.

"Well, hell," I said, "I could use a quick toke."

He proffered a skinny-ass joint from his pocket. "Van's

right over there, if that's cool."

I looked, saw several parked within a hundred yards. "That's cool. Appreciate it."

And off we went.

It's weird, how clearly I remember that final trek across the dirt and gravel. How loud everything sounded. How alert my senses felt. It was like I was stoned already, walking beside him, the sun angled in just such a way that his tall man shadow draped over me. Like his smile was suddenly my umbrella. I remember thinking that, and being mildly amused.

But was I scared? Not even a little. I just wished I was wearing different shoes, different clothes, wasn't dressed for work. Didn't want any grief when I got back. Didn't need any busybody shit. When I looked around and saw nobody, my only thought was, "Oh, thank God."

We passed a van, came up on another, its bashed-in front grill pointed toward us. This got my hopes up, but we walked alongside it without stopping or slowing. The next van was a good fifty yards away. I started to get concerned.

"I'm back on in fifteen minutes, just to be clear," I said.

"Uh-huh," he said, just as we reached the back of the van.

I heard him stop, a split-second before I did.

And there she was, beside the open back door.

I took in the bleached blonde hair, bulging halter top, cut-off jeans at hot-pants length. Saw the dimpled legs and beer-bloat midriff, almost rivaling her boobs. Saw the garish trailer tramp makeup, red lips so huge and crudely drawn they looked clownish themselves. Saw her crappy tattoos.

But mostly what I noted was her terror, at the sight of me. The high-beam crazy of her eyes.

"Omigod! Omigod! HIT HIM, JERRY!" she screamed.

This he did. From behind.

That was my last glimpse of sky.

***

I ain't afraid of you...

The world came back to me, black and cold, throbbing with pain and something worse underneath. I felt it before I felt the floor, heard the faint clink of metal so close to my ears. I felt it in my bones, like they'd been first to awaken.

You can't scare me no more...

That feeling was doom.

It was in me before my eyes flickered open, saw the harsh strobing light and squeezed shut again. It was soaked into my bones before I could smell the dankness, taste the concrete and dust on my tongue.

"Ever since I was little," droned the little girl voice, coming in clearer as my senses caught up, "I been petrified of you. Like I couldn't even move, I felt so frickin' helpless and scared...."

I groaned and stirred, felt the tug and the weight, the clamps tight around my wrists.

"I would wake up from nightmares, and you would be there. Still there. Like the dream coughed you up, left you hangin' up over my bed. Lookin' down. Lookin' down at me and laughin'."

"Oh, no, no," I croaked, more reflex than intention.

"But them days are over. Ain't gonna be like that no more."

I opened my eyes, saw the shackles on my polka-dot sleeves. Saw the shiny red ridge of the squeezable ball on the tip of my nose.

And it all came horribly clear.

"Oh, no, no, no," I said, rising up with a clatter. Rising up only as high as my knees before the chains went taut and yanked me back. I looked around. Saw the chains. Saw the bars of my cage.

Saw the girl recoil, as I faced her at last.

"I AIN'T AFRAID OF YOU!" she shrieked in her little girl squeak, though she had to be thirty at least.

"No, no, no!" I yelled back. "C'mon! You gotta be kiddin'! I mean, what the fuck did *I* do?"

"Oh, you *know* what you did!"

"I didn't do *anything*, lady! I ride a fucking unicycle! I get hit in the face with pies! I give out balloons to kids! Not monster balloons! Just regular ones!"

"*Jerry?*" she screeched, gaze flailing everywhere but me.

"Honest to God, I make less than you make if you work at Walmart! I have no power over anyone! My life is total shit!"

"*Jerry!*" In a panic now.

"I mean, Christ! I was probably just out of high school when you saw Stephen King's *It*, or whatever the fuck happened! But lemme tell you something: CIRCUS CLOWNS ARE JUST PEOPLE! We just wanna make you laugh! It's a job, fercrissake!"

I heard footsteps thunder down the stairs, like two bowling balls racing each other. For one measly moment, I entertained hope. Maybe cops. A nice S.W.A.T. team or three.

"JERRY!"

"*I'm comin', baby!*" called the voice I feared most.

And that was that. So much for hope. I caught my reflection on the shackle on my wrist, saw the white face and red lips, my own warped and desperate eyes.

"Dude!" I hollered. "PLEASE! Come on! It's just me! We were gonna get high!"

I brought my sleeve up, wiped the makeup from one cheek. It came off in a greasepaint smear.

"See? *This is not my face!*"

"JERRY!"

"I'm just a guy! We probably like the same movies! *Look!*" I rubbed my other cheek pink, popped the ball off my nose.

Jerry hit the cage door running.

Then he came in, and cut out my tongue.

***

I cry all the time now. It's pretty much what I do. Cry and whimper, scream and moan. I spend most of my time in the fetal position, while my mind races and my body quakes.

I think about all the things I never did. All the places I never went, and never will. All the girls I never kissed. All the jokes I never made. All the weed I never smoked. On and on and on and on.

Sometimes, I helplessly fantasize about my missing person report. Imagine someone's looking for me. That's the cruelest one of all. I was a transient before I joined the circus. Guys like me come and go, from job to job. One day we show up and audition. A little juggling, a couple pratfalls, and we're on the team. From there, we hang in for as long as it's good, often vanish just as quickly as we came.

I'm not saying they didn't notice me gone, and maybe even miss me a little. I'm just sayin' odds are good that nobody thought, "Someone kidnapped our clown in the parking lot," and put out an APB.

Thinking these thoughts just drives the doom in deeper.

The only close-to-good thoughts are of death, or revenge.

Every day, she comes down and faces her demon. The fact that I'm not one was always way beside the point. It's a matter of pride for her. To see me so weak makes her feel strong.

I'm her totem. Her placebo. Her triumph of the will. I'm the surrogate for everyone that ever wronged her, every Evil Clown movie she ever saw. I'm the reason for her baby-voiced arrested development. The source of all her soul's scar tissue.

And she is making me pay for it all.

That's where Jerry comes in.

The first thing he did after cutting out my tongue was to sew that rubber ball back on the end of my nose. "Nuh-uh-uh," he said, grinning, as the needle dug in. "You don't get off that easy."

Then he carefully affixed these massively-padded Mickey Mouse gloves to my wrists with fishing line, careful not to pop a vein. So that my fingers were buried inside those four cartoon fingers, unable to pry the stitching loose. Fight back. Or tear my own throat out, as the case may be.

She has me all day, to drop in on at will, in between whatever snacks, sex toys, and reality TV she wiles away the rest on. Insofar as I can tell, she never leaves the damn house.

But at night, Jerry comes home. And I am his project.

Every night, after work, he drags me back to the chair.

Every night, he tattoos a little more of my face.

He could have done it all at once, but he's taking his

time. This is clearly his favorite part of the day. Just the white took two months. He spent three weeks on the lips. Now he's rouging my cheeks. And I know the eyes are next.

Fuck if I don't spend every second in that chair just wanting to kill him, over and over. Him and his stupid girlfriend. I wrap the chains around their necks. I stick the needles in their eyes. I taunt, torment, and torture them. Eye for eye. Nose for nose. Limb for limb. Cell by cell.

Meanwhile, I shit down a drain in the concrete floor that is my bed and only home. He cut a trap door in my clown suit, left my raw ass exposed. Every so often, they hose us down. I shiver for days, reek of mildew and sweat. I itch and I ache. And it goes on forever.

So forgive me if I'm fucking depressed.

I look at the corn dog. Only parts of it are green. I sadly thank God I can no longer taste. The last meal I had was cotton candy and gravel, topped with popcorn so stale it broke the last of my teeth.

I think to myself, *should I eat that thing?* There's a part of me that dearly wants to die. Move on. Be free. Reincarnate as a bug, dog, or tree. If there's nothing beyond, just black on black, that's still gotta be way the hell better than this.

I have long given up on Heaven.

But part of me stubbornly wants to live. Knows that something miraculous could happen. A lapse of security. An emotional breakthrough. Revelation. Opportunity... You just never know.

Philosophically speaking, in my dreamiest dreams, I'd love to think I could someday help them see the light. Exorcise this idiotic clown demon. Cut through their psychosis. Transubstantiate the fear. Steer a path toward healing redemption.

But mostly, I just want to rip their fucking throats out, and shit down their necks.

I ain't afraid of you, she says daily, like a mantra.

Oh, but you should be, I think, more and more.

It's the closest to a demon that I will ever get.

And that's how scary clowns are made.

ROSE GOES SHOPPING

Nothing makes you hungry like a zombie apocalypse. Everybody's eating. You can really feel left out.

I'd never been one to stock the pantry overmuch. It just encourages gluttony, the Deadliest Sin to my assline, and a really bad habit by any standard. I'm more of a nibbler, myself. *One bite of a thousand sandwiches*, as Richard used to say, before becoming one expensively over-dressed sandwich for a dozen bitey dead.

Right up until about three minutes ago, Richard was an oily Hollywood agent who clearly slipped on his own personality, in those final moments, when *who he knew* (in a showbiz sense) became dramatically less important than who he was suddenly stuck in a room with.

And screaming at idiots that he thought were beneath him took on a whole new meaning.

I always kind of liked him, though. He was mordant and

sleazy and bluntly funny, utterly shameless in his conniving weaselry. And also, he really liked my show. Purchased lots of pinup posters. (His fetish, he said, was "hot and funny." You gotta admit, there are worse ones to have.)

Which is why he kept coming around, offering me stupid "acting" jobs he hoped might somehow get me to fuck him. Wasn't gonna happen, but you kind of have to admire tenacity… which I would consider to be one of the "Ten Deadly Skills," though these are tellingly not revealed in the Bible.

That said, neither were the "Seven Deadly Sins," and nobody ever seems to shut up about *them*.

Anyway, I'm thinking about Richard because a) they're eating him, about thirty feet away, and b) despite that, I'm still really hungry, and c) I'm also still in the goddam bodega, trying to figure out how to vamoose with this food before they figure out I'm here.

There are three aisles in Paco's Carniceria, running front-to-back in the traditional manner. I am at the back, in the dairy section, quietly loading cheese into my overflowing plastic basket. It's really hard not to just peel one wrapper, take a couple quick chomps to tide me over. But that would just be stupid. If they didn't hear the noise, they might smell the fresh aroma.

Fucking zombies.

They complicate everything.

I have two environmentally conscious hemp-woven grocery bags already packed. This shit is getting really heavy. But I don't know how many more chances I will have.

Making good on payment is probably not an issue, since three of the dead are behind the counter, chowing down on

Paco, God rest his soul. They actually came right over the counter at him. It all went down so fast.

The biggest problem is Richard, who chose to flip out and be a total asshole right in front of the front door. THANKS, RICHARD!

I consider my options.

Theoretically, I could duck out the back, behind the meat counter, maybe pick up some weapons and pork chops along the way. But someone's banging on that door already. And somehow, I don't think it's the cops.

On the other hand, the storefront window is wide. I could bust it open, drop the bags outside, sweep the broken glass from the frames, vault over, and hit the pavement on the run with relative ease.

The problem being that I don't know who I'd meet out there. Or how many.

And there are zombies in aisles One, Two, *and* Three.

They're distracted by pieces of Richard, or the other guy they took down in the dog food section. It's a miracle they haven't gotten to me yet.

As a big fan of miracles, surrounded by bounty, I find this immensely encouraging.

I sidle away from Aisle One, with its beeline to the door—closing the glass fridge door with utmost care—and take a silent peek at Aisle Two. Only one down there. A teenage black girl. Kind of awkward. Kind of cute. I like her shoes, the nerdy glasses still half-dangling off her chubby lifeless face.

Awww, I think. She makes me sadder than Richard. She was probably actually nice, in real life.

But she has a chunk of someone in her hands—I'm

guessing organ meat, by the glistening grayness—that seems to have her full attention. She's barely looking at the rolls of toilet paper she will never use again.

I seize the opportunity, duck past to Aisle Three.

Three is the number. That's how many are there, not counting the victim.

But you know what else is there, halfway up the aisle, as abandoned as life?

A shopping cart. More encouraging news.

A plan takes form inside my mind.

I think about setting down the basket, immediately rule against it. I'll be a little bit noisier and slower at first; but once the cart starts rolling, all bets are off anyway. That's one less step I have to take, once I have everyone's attention.

I look back at the bags, like how they're positioned. Consider that this may be the last stupid trick I ever pull. Either way, once the clock starts ticking, I have maybe a minute to either pull this off or not.

Okay. I clock my moves in advance, rehearse my strategy step-by-step. It takes this many seconds from there to there. A second for this. A second for that. Maybe ten seconds for the next bit. Three seconds to transition.

Then bing-bang-bing-bang boom boom boom.

Can I do it?

I don't know.

With my back to the shelves between aisles Two and Three, I see myself reflected in refrigerator glass. I look like an anime cartoon character, preposterously colorful in my electric green streetfighting jumpsuit, red bouffant wig and matching boots.

Behind my reflection hang rows and rows of assorted

lunchmeats, pre-sliced and neatly packaged. Already dead meats, hoping someone will eat them, so that their deaths were not a total fucking waste.

I could be one of those meats, resign myself to that fate, if I believed for a second that being eaten by these dimwits would in any way validate my death. Like feeding the newborn zombie race would somehow ennoble them, raise them up from their humble beginnings to a greater, more soulful understanding, eventually surpassing the civilizations they are now poised to topple…

But that ain't gonna happen.

That ain't gonna happen, cuz the bottom line is this: *zombies are us with nothing left to offer.* They're us when all of the light, and the point, are gone. In the hour and a half since I was forced to re-kill the first one I saw, they have proven this over and over.

These dumb motherfuckers wouldn't even know who they were eating. They don't know who they're eating now. They don't even bother to digest us, I'm guessing. Tearing us apart and then chewing us up is just something to do: the only game left in town that they still know how to play.

I look in the eyes of my reflection, and remember what it was like to have no one there looking back at me. When I was staring back at lithium and Prozac and so many state-sanctioned, soul-deadening prescription drugs that I barely even recognized the blank face, the dank hair and smeared makeup that ovaled around those utterly empty mirrors of my soul.

When I couldn't even see myself, looking straight at myself, for hours on end.

That's what the zombies have to offer me. That's the best

45

they have to offer to anyone. They're like Dr. Skullfuck's wettest dream, taking over the world at last.

I take a deep breath, smile back at my reflection. This entire reverie has taken roughly three seconds. You think a lot of things fast, in moments of crisis like these.

So, once again…

Can I do this?

I'm about to find out.

I step into Aisle Three, and the clock starts ticking. The shopping cart is roughly fifteen feet away. *Clop clop clop* go my cherry red steel-toed construction boots, just as quiet as I can be. The cart is tilted with the handle away at one o'clock. I'll have to grab it from the front and pull.

Hard as I try to be quiet, the goodies in my pic-a-nic basket provide just enough rustle and clatter to make one of the dead look up as I close in on the cart, now only three feet away. I consider this a victory.

By the time he starts to rise, I plop the basket in the cart, start wheeling it back toward me, walking backwards fast.

This is the first five seconds.

By second ten, I have pulled around to Aisle Two, aimed the cart straight ahead like an arrow. Then a quick dance to the left, twisting fully around, feet planted and knees bent before I pick up the heavy bags. The last thing I need is to throw out my back with an awkward maneuver. I have to move fast. And I have to be strong.

I lift and toss the bags into the cart. They feel light, inside the adrenaline rush of panic. The convoy is fully loaded.

Now's when I take a couple extra seconds to bait the trap.

"WHO'S HUNNNNNGRY?" I bellow down Aisle One, and do a little evocative dance.

As one, the eaters of Richard ascend, distracted from their feeding by my fresh wiggly meat. I make sure they're all upright before ducking out of sight.

Another deep breath. Counting one, two, three.

Then I grab the cart by the handle and stampede straight up Aisle Two, directly toward my poor teenage friend, who has noticed me at last. Cute as she is, her eyes are blank. There is no one to relate to as I mow her down, then let go of the cart.

And throw all my weight into pushing against the shelves to my right.

It's amazing how easily they go over. I would blame cheap construction if I weren't so goddam grateful. They were built for mobility, and never properly anchored in. Like a film set, thrown up only to be torn down. No sense of permanence.

KABOOM.

I hear the lead zombie pulp under the cacophonous onslaught of cans and glass and metal shelves, violently cascading down. Not a solid squish, but wet and crunchy all the same. He won't be getting up any time soon.

My sweet little teen is half-pinned under the cart. I'm concerned that she might upset it. So I blow her a kiss, tell her I'm sorry, and stab her in the eye with a steak knife I grabbed from Housewares. She stops moving right away.

Then I stand, pushing over the shelves on the left.

So much for the back of aisles One and Three.

I don't know how many of them I just flattened, don't have time to check. I'm the kind of person who notices things, and one thing I'd noticed in my years shopping here is that Paco's shelves were sectioned into thirds. I hurtle myself once again to the right, hit the center section.

It starts to keel over, then keels over all the way.

I can hear the zombie uproar over the actual uproar of shit keeling over, then careen to the left, and repeat the procedure. More shelves coming down. More undead yammer.

Time to take one last push to the right, marking the end of Aisle Three as we know it. There's a satisfying thwonk to the cans careening. I hear a former someone groan, as the goods rain down upon 'em. If it's not enough to kill them again, it's certainly a start.

The shelves go BOOM. The groaning stops.

And then—with but one section left to topple—a massive drooling cholo rounds what's left of Aisle One and steps into my path, less than six feet away.

In the world that just ended roughly ninety-six minutes ago, by my count, this guy must have been gangbanger muscle. Not much taller than me, but built like a freight locker: twice as wide, and easily two hundred pounds heavier. His prison tattoos flow from his neck to his wrists, much like the blood covering all those same areas. Looks like somebody bit off his Adam's apple.

But now he's looking at me.

"FUCK A DUCK!" I hear myself say, but I am already moving. No time to waste on fear. In a perfect world, I guess he'd have waddled into my previous traps. But they probably would have just bounced right off him.

I pluck a can of Dinty Moore Beef Stew off one of the last remaining shelves, wing it straight at his head. It misses, goes straight out the window. Which begins the shattering process, but does not resolve this situation.

He shambles closer, and a thick glob of semi-chewed Richard falls out of the hole in his neck, the mouth and wound alike smeared redder than the world's worst nightmare clown.

I pluck another Dinty Moore, wind up, and pitch.

It nails him straight in the forehead, and he staggers back a foot, then surges forward some more.

FUCK!

I could lob crappy food at his head all day, and he'd probably just keep coming. I can feel the seconds ticking, my chances slipping away. I could try to duck around him, but then what about *my* food?

I need a better idea, fast.

I get one.

I laugh.

The shopping cart is ten feet behind me. I race back toward it so fast I can't count the seconds, and start the clock again. Pushing the cart back off the dead girl, grabbing it by the front again, then pulling it in front of me, and grabbing hold of the handle hard.

Ramming him straight on and knocking him flat would just thoroughly block my exit. But the absence of Aisle Three gives me just enough width to veer slightly to the right as I'm building up speed.

And then come back at him sideways, at an angle, as hard as I possibly can.

His arms rear up, but nowhere near the cart itself, which catches him full in his left love handles and topples him into the last remaining shelves of Aisle One.

They could not possibly cave in faster.

That fucker is *fat*.

And I am on my way.

For the first time, the front door seems strangely accessible. I steer wildly toward it, in the newly-opened space...

...and all that remains between me and there is Richard.

He is looking at me.

There is not a lot left of his face. And there is nothing left of his personality. If I didn't know where I am, and what's happening... if I didn't recognize his suit and remaining hair...

...if I hadn't just run into this store with him, mere minutes ago: me trying to convince him that this zombie shit was real, and that stocking up was of the essence, while we still could...

...and him humoring me, only tagging along because he so desperately wanted to bang me...

...well, I wouldn't even know it was him at all.

But I know who he was. And he's looking at me, with just one eyeball left. And the hunger in its gaze is not so far removed from the one I always recognized there. *Always* recognized there. Cuz there was no mistaking it.

"Sorry, Richard," I say. "None for you."

What's left of his left arm grapples toward me, wet fingertips tickling my calf from beneath the cart as I finish rolling over it like a speed bump. It's the closest he ever got to feeling me up. I only wish he could enjoy it as little as I am.

Then I am back on the street again.

The Los Angeles sun is beating down hard. It's the middle of the fucking afternoon. Horror is not supposed to play in broad daylight.

But here it is, in its own way far darker than night.

There's a car on fire, as I wheel down the street. The one that it collided with has not, as yet, ignited. But it will. I just hope I'm closer to home before it goes up.

Because the fire is attracting them, like ugly moths to death's flame.

And of course there are no cops, no emergency vehicles showing up to contain this little glitch in the cosmic system. We live on the ugly industrial outskirts of godforsaken downtown L.A. Nobody gives a shit about us. Didn't then. Don't now. Won't ever. We are the poor, the lost and disenfranchised.

And we are totally on our own.

There are still cars moving on the 6th Street Bridge, but they ain't movin' fast. Not as fast as they'd like.

And there are people on the bridge that are no longer people, if I were to hazard a guess. Closing in on those cars. Waiting for traffic to fully jam.

This is just getting worse and worse.

I roll forward, rounding the bend onto Jesse St., and nobody gets in my way. I see no other living people. All the rest are dead and busily feeding, or meandering about, like a game of Marco Polo after everybody drowned.

Fortunately, this is not a very populous neighborhood. And thank God it's a Saturday, so all the industrial buildings are shut down for the weekend. Shit is pretty spread out, which gives me plenty of room to move.

It isn't until I'm a block from my home that a serious obstacle comes up.

I see him before he sees me, but I don't like what I see. He, on the other hand, seems to like me too much; and I'm quite certain that, in life, it would have been much the same.

He was a construction worker or something—he's got a hardhat on his head—and he's big, and he's buff, and he's scary as fuck. From the look of his arms, he could have bench-pressed that fat cholo. In his tight, revealing tank top, you can see his six-pack abs, even through all the blood. And there is a lot. Definitely the winner so far in the Wet Zombie T-Shirt competition (Male category).

He's ahead of me by roughly 100 yards, and way off to my left. He's performed a taffy pull on somebody's small intestine, seems to have all thirty feet of it draped and dangling from his hands.

When he sees me, he does not stop his noshing. He just drags them along behind him, growling with his mouth full, on a total intercept course.

I'm not sure what to do about this. With a guy like that, I'm gonna need a gun. And I don't have one. Not at home, and not here.

I think about doubling back, taking a side street, and going around the block. But who knows what I'll run into there? I'm so close. I'm so close…

All the while, he is coming closer.

Right then, a silver SUV comes whipping around the corner two blocks down, tires squealing as it heads directly for me. I let go of the cart, jump up and down, waving my arms like I have pom-poms for hands. I feel like the last cheerleader of the human race.

"I'M ALIVE!" I holler, even though they can't hear me. "LOOK! I'M ALIVE!"

The SUV doesn't slow down.

I start to wonder if I should pull over, toward the curb on the right-hand side. But if they drive right past me, I'm right back where I was. I could use a little help, is the fact of the matter.

I stand my ground, and hope to God they don't just run me down.

Mr. Zombie Universe turns to watch, as well. He doesn't stop coming, but he's aware that something's up. He seems a little *too* aware, if you ask me. Like he lost his soul, but not his cunning.

Meanwhile, the SUV keeps coming.

I'm no longer sure who I'm scared of more.

Save the food, says the sanest of the voices in my head; and before I think to argue, I am doing what it says, skedaddling off to the right as the vehicle closes in.

Veers toward me.

And then screeches to a halt.

I can hear them laughing, from the wheel and shotgun seats. Can see them through the windshield. Am pretty sure it's just the two.

They are assholes in escape mode: probably cracked out, clearly out of their minds. I'm pretty sure these wheels are stolen, and this is their end-of-the-world joyride.

The front doors fly open to either side, and out come the Bobsy Twins, going "WOOOO!" with their newfound manly power. Mr. Shotgun doesn't have one, but he has a baseball bat. Captain Driver has some sort of serious handgun I'm not quite close enough to gauge.

"Don't you worry, little lady!" Captain Handgun slurs. It's supposed to be commanding, but he lists to one side. Drunk *and* cracked out? Wouldn't be a first, 'round these parts.

"Thanks!" I say. "I was starting to wonder."

"Get in," says Baseball Batman. "We're gonna take good care of you."

"No, that's cool," I say. "I'm just on my way home…"

"What, are you *stupid?*" he continues. "Get in!"

This jangles my nerves no end. I could fit this guy's IQ in a contact lens. We all know where this is heading. Fucked by morons till I'm dead.

And right there, I make my decision: *no way* are these simpletons eating all my chocolate and cheese. I throw up my hands, thrust my boobs out, smile sweetly.

And take a hard look around at everything but them.

The hardhatted zombie is getting closer. A couple others have perked up, as well. In another ten to twenty seconds, this could easily turn into one against two against six.

"I'm sorry," I half-lie. "I've got children to feed."

"That looks like a lot of good food," says Captain Capgun.

"Yeah, I know! There's a store, like, three blocks back…"

"No," he says. "That looks…" Mind stuttering for a second, pointing at the cart. "We'll just take that."

"Oh, come on!" I say, pushing the cart closer to him. "You don't know what I just went through! I killed every zombie in the goddam place, and there's still enough food there to feed you for months!"

Off to my left, the Mr. Universe of zombies is getting close enough to start making Batman visibly fidget. He keeps looking back and forth between me and Mr. Universe, me and Mr. Universe. And that long trail of dragging gut sausage behind him.

I'm starting to like the fact that the SUV is blocking each other's rear view. They can both see me—and they can see each other—but they can't watch each other's back.

But me—standing smack-dab in the center—I am seeing it all. And my smile is getting wider by the second.

"Fuck going to the store!" says the guy with the gun. "You comin' or not?"

I can't help it. I start laughing, and stare straight at his crotch. Which, I note, is already pre-moistened.

You ever want to unnerve a man, just stare at his crotch and laugh.

"Fuck this!" bellows Batboy, pointing his bat at Alpha Zombie. "SHOOT THIS FUCKING THING, GARY!"

"Shoot WHAT fucking thing?" Gary says, as he turns his gaze through the SUV's side windows...

...and I push forward, with all my might...

...and I'm three feet away before he turns to look back at me, two feet away before he starts to aim his gun, precisely one shopping cart away before he actually pulls the trigger.

Missing wildly, as I plow that asshole down.

I stop on a dime, do not roll him over, racing around the cart as the gun skitters from his hand. The back of his skull hits the pavement hard, making his eyes as glassy as those of the dead.

I give Gary a steel-toed kick in the teeth, just to fuck him up harder. Then I kick him in the nose, hear it shatter, hear him scream.

On the other side of the SUV, I hear Batboy scream as well, sneak a sidelong glance through the windows: just long enough to see him locked in a tug of war over the bat. The buffed-up Alpha Zombie holds the fat end in both hands, and is reeling that poor stupid bastard in so fast he forgets to let go of the grip.

I see all this in one split-second, and think, *omigod. That thing CAUGHT THE BAT IN MID-SWING...*

But I don't have time to think about this. The clock has

not stopped ticking. The gun is on the pavement. I pick it up, don't recognize the brand.

I look around to see four zombies converging. Shoot the closest one in the head. It works.

Captain Pavement tries to get to his feet. I weigh the morality for a second—contemplate the taking of a human life—then blow a hole where his right nipple used to be. He goes right back down, just the way I like him.

Gary's moist eyes look suddenly human.

But I'm not fooled for a second.

"Guys like you," I say, "make me root for the zombies."

He calls me a cunt.

Which tells me all I need to know.

I don't know how many more bullets are left in this gun, but I ain't about to waste 'em on his sorry ass. If there's anything left of him to come back and bug me later, I'll take care of it then. But frankly, I'm skeptical.

That boy looks like zombie food to me.

Same for his little buddy, who I can no longer see. But it's amazing how loudly he's coming apart.

I'm amazed that I'm still hungry.

Inside the cart, there are rice and beans and pasta and cheese and salsa enough to survive for weeks. I wish I'd grabbed some of those pre-packaged lunchmeats, but whaddaya gonna do? It was a spur of the moment thing.

I did grab lots of cookie dough and chocolate, though. Cuz God knows we need cookies. And coffee. And milk. (I also got coffee and milk.)

And I gotta admit, I splurged a little. Were this not the zombie apocalypse, I might have held back on the anchovies, Spanish olives, artichoke hearts, hearts of palm and such.

But they're all minor delicacies I've always enjoyed, and can rarely afford.

Under the circumstances, fuck it.

If I have to die horribly, I at least deserve a little oddball scrumptiousness. Don'tcha think?

I DO!

And so, once again, I roll down lonesome Jesse St., easily dodging the rest of the lumbering dead. Thanking God they're so slow, so devoid of spark or fire.

Weirdly thanking God for the distraction created by those drugged-out shitwits, who only meant to do me harm. (Talk about working in mysterious ways!)

And praying to God, while I'm at it, that I don't run into Mr. Wet T-Shirt Contest again. Back-asswards, he totally saved mine. But I can't help but feel he was just saving it for later.

Which is why I will reserve one bullet for him, no matter what. And hope somebody knocks that hardhat off him, before we meet again. A clean shot would make all the difference.

Unless, of course, he can also catch bullets in his hand...

Before I know it, I am back at my building, where all of my friends are waiting. They're not children, exactly. But in the grand scheme of things, they are all extremely small. They will want to hear every detail, much as it will scare and pain them.

They will want me to tell them the truth.

I think that's my job, from now on.

At the curb, Richard's car is parked. A lipstick-red 2007 Maserati GranSport convertible. What a douche. If this were any other time but this, that thing would have been stolen by now. At least in this neighborhood.

I kick a couple dents in the driver's side, just to make it fit in. I don't want anyone thinking there's money in this building. The paint flecks spackle my boot with snappy sparkle. It looks really pretty. I kick with the other foot, till they match. Maybe I'll emboss it on, later.

I think about tearing the top, taking out a turn signal light or something. But nah. Worse come to worst, I might possibly need it later. And at least I'll always know where the keys are.

Nobody leaps from the shadows as I enter the indoor parking garage, curse the fact that the metal drop-down gate is still broken. Fucking landlord. Fucking zombies. Fucking fuck. This is a space that will get hard to defend. Sad but true.

But it's all good, for the moment. Yelling "HEY! IT'S ME!" three seconds before I knock on the door, do my signature drum roll. Letting them know it's me.

The door opens at once. It's Danny, my cameraman and bestest friend. I was hoping he'd make it here okay.

"Oh, THANK GOD!" he says, sweeping me up in a hug.

"I already did!" I say, laughing, hugging him back.

Then we roll the cart full of life-giving goodies inside, shut and lock the door behind us.

Nothing makes you hungry like a zombie apocalypse.

"Let's eat!" I say.

Worm Central Tonite!

So I'm burrowing into this dead guy's eyeball, having dispensed with the lid-flap at last. Hard work. Painstaking. Tough to dissolve.

But tasty? Yes.

Worth the effort? Absolutely.

A little perspective is a wonderful thing.

For example:

I'm not a big eater, but I do love to eat. I mean, sure, I shit my own body weight daily. But as graveyard worms go, I am fairly svelte.

Not like Braxis, already plowing straight through the glazed pupil beside me like an animate sausage arrow in relentless bullseye mode. That guy is so fucking fat he can barely undulate without popping his casing, but away he goes, tail flipping past my face, riding the gravy train straight down the optic nerve railroad.

He will beat me to the brain, no question.

He always does.

There's a lot of traffic at Worm Central tonite. Fresh meat. Always a cause for celebration. People haven't been dying fast enough lately. I've got a bad feeling this dustbowl town is drying up.

But here in the socket, pushing through to the goo, things couldn't be more moist and juicy. I could wallow in here all day. I love those moments when I see how they see as a *pure experience*, disconnected from the conclusions they draw one micro-instant later, when the rest of the relays kick in.

But there is no substitute for the Big Picture.

As such, I squirm through, swallowing just enough to show me blue skies in a green world. The last sights they saw, before closing forever.

Then I'm squeezing through the cracks in the bone—somebody definitely took a hammer to this clown—and on my way to the main course.

Most of the worms I know like to soak in muscle memory. What it felt like to have arms. What it felt like to have legs. Some are all about the genitalia, those uncanny vibrations. (I went through that phase.)

Some mystics seek out the heart, in search of love. I tried that, too.

Most head straight for the guts, and what they know. Being none the wiser is fine with them.

Me, I like to know what it was like to grapple with it all. To have ALL those things going on at once. To have words to describe it.

Again: a little perspective is a wonderful thing.

But to each their own. Tonight, we dine. Riddling this otherwise-empty vessel with the only life it will ever know again.

Remembered, one bite at a time.

Tonight, I will learn how this poor bastard lived. How he died. How much TV he watched. How much he hated his job. How much he got laid. How many people he hurt. How many times he smiled and meant it.

What he thought about his place here on Earth.

Not a bad gig for a worm, all told.

I slither after Braxis, grab my front row seat, take a big bite of cerebral DNA…

…and the first thing I taste is his fear, the wild synapse-flashes of his meat's impending end. It combines with the eyeball-memory of the swing and connect, a hammer indeed, cracking skull and yanking bone back out, the claw end wet and caked and red…

Very scary. No doubt about it. In terms of intensity, it beats the fuck out of *Scarface:* a movie this dimwit clearly loved.

But here's the thing. *The end is the end*, every meat-go-round. I will die soon, too. Just another squiggly vessel.

But my memories will pass on. From flesh to flesh to flesh.

No real end.

And no forgetting.

As such, I snuggle into the cranial folds. Chew past the terror-bites, as they gradually give way to deeper, more rewarding bounty.

Just another night in Worm Central.

Forever and ever.

Amen.

Skipp's Hollywood Alphabet Soup of Horror

A IS FOR ALPHA

Above, somethings slither with ponderous weight.

Below, they are tearing off pounds at a time.

In the stands that surround the blood pit, the Audience leans forward as if their heads were every bit as heavy, watching as the man with the ancient Oscar takes a swing at the kid lining up for nomination, the statue's skull a jagged thing that severs as it thuds.

The kid is good—his last three pictures made money, and his blade cuts swift and deep—but the chunk of skull that crunches free at this moment lets just a little too much air in, directly on the brain.

He crumples, spraying, and already praying that the next project won't be this fucking hard. Maybe a sequel wouldn't be so bad, after all. Got to be better than this.

The elder survives, maimed and poked full of holes, but gets to fight one more heavyweight A-list round.

Approval gurgles, unearthly, from the rafters, where the real decisions are made.

Barely heard, above the Audience's hypnotized cheers.

B IS FOR BIG OPENING WEEKEND

When the 100 million dollar remake of *It Conquered the World* didn't, it was a disaster to end all disaster movies. Not since the epic fail of the Matthew Broderick *Godzilla* had a monster so huge fallen so short of expectations.

They'd made billboards of skyscrapers, plastered every bus in L.A. with the creature's odious eyes, put John Hamm and Harrison Ford on every talk show in existence. It wasn't enough. *It* finished eighth, with a weekend gross of $3.6 mil. The talking hamster film took sixth.

So when the flying saucers appeared over Hollywood Way in Burbank on Sunday, many suspected it was a last-ditch effort by Warner Bros. to pump some life into the thing.

But when the beams of searing power rained down from above to liquefy the water tower, raze the sound stages, and carbonize Bryan Singer, it was time to guess again.

Turns out that the aliens were just as sick of big-budget miss-the-point bullshit as everyone else.

On the other hand, the Discovery Channel has gotten reeeeeal popular, all of a sudden.

C IS FOR CREDIT

It's worth its weightlessness in gold.
(Or, at least, so I've been told.)
That's why they'll slice and gut you clean
To see their names up on the screen.

D IS FOR DIRECTORIAL DECISION-MAKING

Derek's got the shot all figured out. He's worked with his DP and production designer for months, in pre-production, visualizing every speck of the scene. Choreographing every camera move. Rehearsing on computer, in pre-vis, so that the hundreds of extras mill about in just the right ways as the helicopter zooms in over the villa, stops to hover overhead, then gently lowers our POV down toward their upturned faces (a Steadi-rig lowered to a waiting cameraman on a rooftop, who snuggles into the harness as a stuntman pretends to grapple with the villainous Dieter Meyer: our suggested point of view).

The camera then head-butts the stuntman and runs down the stairs, past apartments whose doors fly open, extras cowering as it passes, one after another, whipping from floor to floor to floor until the front door looms at the end of the corridor that we whip toward, then kick our way through, out into the street.

The crowd parts, and Dieter (the camera) plows forward, up the plaza and around the bend, past dozens of persuasively terrified extras and our leading lady before closing in on Daniel Day-Lewis—a hero, this time—

surging forward to *collide with the camera...*

All in one unbroken shot.

What could possibly go wrong?

Well...

The cable snaps, as the camera's lowered. It falls fast, straight on the head of the cameraman, whose skull caves in as he buckles to his knees, the footage still rolling...

...and the stuntman wrenches the camera free, proceeds to do what he's watched the cameraman do a hundred times in rehearsal, running through the door and down the stairs and into the street, then through the crowd, turning right where he's supposed to...

...just as the helicopter crashes into the street before him, extras ducking and diving and crunching beneath it, blades hacking through the last resistant limbs before the engine ignites, and the fireball plumes...

...and the camera catches it all, in the seconds before the stuntman is blown back, upside down, and out.

Just long enough to see what happens to our star.

It's stupendous.

Only then does Derek yell, "CUT!"

E IS FOR EGO

I am who I say that I am. And whatever I believe myself to be is precisely what I'll be.

There is nothing I can't accomplish, no goal I can set that can't be met. No sight is too high. No prize out of reach.

If I can picture it, it is already mine.

I am broken inside, and I came to this town to prove that I was someone. Someone special. Someone with something to say. The place that I came from had no use for me. They didn't get me. They didn't want me. I couldn't get laid to save my life.

But I've shown them. *I accomplished, baby.* I did the thing I said I'd do. They can't turn on the TV without running the risk of seeing me there. Bigger than life. Bigger than them. Being seen. Being heard.

Being remembered.

While they are forgotten.

And I say to myself, "Who the fuck are you? I know famous people. I *am* famous people! Doesn't it make you sick, knowing that nobody knows who you are, or gives a shit about you, past your handful of stupid friends? Doesn't it make you sick, knowing that millions of people love me? Or at least know who I am? Doesn't that make you hate yourself?"

I hate myself. But I am learning to love. Learning to love the people who say they love me. I love them back. I am grateful. Oh so grateful. Because I am special, and they know it. Not like you.

Not like you.

I am who I say I am.

Please love me.

You wouldn't believe how incredible I am.

F IS FOR FAME

It's the best. Flat-out. Everything they said it was. All it's ever been cracked up to be. All that and more.

The greatest drug in the world.

Once you taste it—*once it tastes you*—no other experience will do. Without it, reality shrinks and constricts like psychic Saran Wrap, gets smaller and grayer and less alive, under tight nerveless skin.

The unseen gods—those that slither through the rafters—secrete it from their vast oily pores. It spoots, pools, and spreads through the Tinseltown vastness overhead, lolls down long organic unearthly Lovecraftian flumes: a black syrup that eventually droozles humanward, one thick invaluable drop at a time.

One spritz of it will turn you for life. To bathe in it is incomparable bliss. And the line to the blood pit is incredibly long.

When they talk about being in the right place at the right time, they are measuring it in droplets of fame.

G IS FOR GOFER

Gary's a gofer (also known as "P.A."):
A production assistant, kept running all day.
If he's not getting this, then he's going for that,
Fulfilling their whims at the drop of a hat.
When he finally drops dead, out of stress and fatigue,
They'll call in for Gus, Mary, Teri, and Teague.
If his sister can't do it, they'll go for his cousin,
Cuz fucking P.A.'s are a dime a dozen.

H IS FOR HEAD SHOT

Hailey works the front desk at Hollywood Head Shot. Her eyes are the questionnaire. She observes the hopefuls as they fill out the form, slaps her x in the appropriate box, and passes it on.

Dr. Harvester scans the form in the moment before the next client comes in. Notes the x, but reserves the right to decide for himself. He shoots celebrities, after all.

Hayden Horowitz enters, takes his seat before the red screen, and assumes the facial position. You always want to open with your winningest smile. But the nose is not right. Sorry, pal. Good call, Hailey.

BOOM. Shot lined up, and wetly taken. Hank comes in to drag him out and put him on the pile out back.

The next girl is gorgeous, and her pictures turn out fine.

I IS FOR INDIE

Every year, thousands of bold renegades and hapless dreamers storm the citadel, hoping to make it past the clamping jaws that are the gates of the Machine.

From idiosyncratic individualists to idiot savants to amateur idealists to I-obsessed cannon-fodder, they feed themselves into the dragon's mouth, hoping to make it down the gullet with their bodies and souls intact.

The blood pits await, for the chosen few.

But most just lube the gates.

J IS FOR JADED

Jason used to love movies. That's why he came.

But every film that succeeded, while all his projects failed, just killed whatever voyeuristic joy he had left.

He still has his standbys—his Kubricks, his Coppolas, his *Casablancas* and *Citizen Kanes*—that he will fight to the death to defend. But they're just bulwarks and bludgeons against the vast unworthiness that constitutes modern cinema today.

Jason drinks a lot, screaming at his TV.

And nary a droplet falls near.

K IS FOR KISSASS

In Hollywood, there are at least a thousand for every successful asshole.

This may help explain why many so many successful Hollywood assholes grow an extra ring of teeth.

L IS FOR THE LUCKIEST MOTHERFUCKERS IN THE WORLD

Their careers have spanned decades, and *defined* those decades, with signature works that illuminated their times, becoming personally and indelibly iconic in the process. Throughout it all, they have maintained a clear commitment to their artistic visions, and their truest selves.

They have found personal peace through following their path, trusting their instincts, and always giving back one thousand percent to their audience. They're so sure of their craft that they're not afraid to help others, guide them through with passion and devotion and honest love for the joy and privilege of the process itself.

They're amazing, they're legends, and we never forget them, long after they have drowned in glorious fame.

You wouldn't believe how many people hate those lucky motherfuckers.

M IS FOR THE MONEY, HONEY

The only thing almost as good as fame.

N IS FOR NO

The most popular word in Hollywood, and the last thing you hear before you die screaming.

O IS FOR OPPORTUNITY KNOCKIN'

"So I'm on the bus, with the rest of the extras, heading out into the Mojave. And everybody else is just bullshitting, talking up how famous they're about to become, or complaining about how hot it's getting, and how cool it would be to duck into your trailer as the star of this stupid movie, instead of burning up like everybody else.

"But I don't even have to listen to know that's what they're saying. The standard yammering blah blah blah. Meanwhile, I'm absorbing the script, which I plucked off of Otto's bootleg site. Figuring out the movie we're being paid $65 a day to stand around in. Getting to know it by heart.

"So we land at the location, and everybody gets wardrobed up. I make sure I'm at the front of the line, so I nab a nice dress, and get to the makeup artists before they're all worn out, and still have time to get my bearings. Make some friends in the crew. Suss out the lay of the land.

"It's the first day of shooting, but the leading lady is already a notorious pain in the ass. Won't come out of her trailer even to check out the location. Making the director come to her. Clearly not learning her lines.

"So the first shot of the day is a crowd scene. And I am right up front, big-boobed and ebullient. The DP likes me, features me in much subsequent coverage. Loves my enthusiasm, my red hair, my tits. He confers with the director, who nods as he smiles and stares.

"Half an hour of this later, it's time for the leading lady to come out. She doesn't. They wait, pick up a couple more B-roll shots. She still doesn't come. A P.A. is sent. Minutes drag by. The tension mounts.

"The P.A. returns, white as cocaine. The leading lady's in a coma. Quite probably drug o.d. Panic hurricanes through the production.

"That's when I walk up to the Director of Photography, tell him that I've memorized the script. He says, "WHAT?" I tell him how. He tells the director. Rinse and repeat.

"Bottom line. I'm the new star of the film. The dumb bitch dies. The publicity is stunning. Plucked out of nowhere, I rise to the challenge, and the top of the field. Rags to riches, overnight.

"So is that luck? No. That's preparation. And that is my advice to you.

"When opportunity knocks, you open the door.

"Open it quietly.

"And don't leave fingerprints."

P IS FOR PRIMA DONNA

There are some people—some extremely popular people—who are not worth going through the motions with.

They're just horrible, horrible human beings. Egos reduced to reflexive scar tissue and a truly deranged sense of boundless entitlement, psychopathic in their ability to project empathy onscreen, while personally having not a speck of their own.

Sometimes, you will have to work with them. Sometimes, it's not so bad. If they fear you enough to respect you, but not so much that they have to destroy you, you can have a really good time with them. If they didn't have talent and charisma and drive, these Donnas would be utterly prima-free.

Polly is a perfect example. She's America's Sweetheart. Her eyes are so blue, her skin is so perfect, her smile so incandescent that boners sproing, and wives mournfully dream of somehow impossibly topping that act.

You don't know how many eyeballs she ate to get just that shade of blue. How many skins she peeled. How many boners she beguiled. How many charms and wiles she gobbled, worked for years to refine and perfect.

Dr. Harvester supplements his income by feeding her the freshest parts. She is entitled to them. Cuz God knows *they* didn't deserve them.

"I try to take a little something from everyone I meet," she says in interviews, with a flash of her pearly whites. She's more than smart enough to know how important that is. She also eats hearts, just to remember how they work.

She is hell on wheels. And we love her to death.

The love is all hers.

And the death is all ours.

Q IS FOR QUITTERS

The line is long, but they're still standing in it, though their knees ache all the way from their hips down through their shins. Belinda leans lightly on Colin's frail shoulder, but a good breeze might easily topple them both.

"You got a light?" says some straggly hipster kid with no right to be here, sidling up beside him.

"Go fuck yourself, Junior," Colin snaps, already turning his back.

"Wow," the kid says. "Really?"

"Wow. Really. Yeah." Colin fires one up, just for spite, starts spontaneously hacking as the smoke hits his one remaining lung.

The kid starts laughing, and Belinda hobbles forward, saying, "You are a very rude young man."

"What?"

"Show a little respect."

"All I wanted was…"

By then, the coughing is under control, and Colin turns back. "Let me ask you something, buddy. How long have you been in line?"

"Almost six months…"

"Whoa. Aren't you the little trooper." Colin hacks and cackles. "You won't last a year."

Colin started young, at his mother's behest. It's been sixty-three years since his first audition. He's seen 'em come and go so many times over you'd think he'd lived lifetimes, just standing still.

Belinda Quinn is younger, but more stooped at the shoulders. Those boobs hadn't gotten any lighter over the last forty years. Less enticing, perhaps.

But that didn't mean you quit.

Up ahead, someone lets out a groan, and a couple of women scream. You can't see through the throngs, but Security moves in; and a couple minutes later, the meat wagon is there.

"Johnny…" goes the whisper up and down the endless line. *"Omigod…it's Johnny Wade…"*

"Such a shame," says Belinda. "He was very talented."

"Quitter," Colin hisses, as they wheel the corpse away.

R IS FOR REWRITES

Robert hands in his draft. It's the fifteenth so far. Only three of them were his: numbers one, three, and this.

They come back to him when they realize they have totally lost their way. That takes a lot of balls, after all they've been through; but one look at Draft Fourteen shows precisely why they need him.

"It's not my monster any more," he says simply. "Everything that was scary about it is gone. All I did was bring it back to what it is."

They agree, tell him they respect his vision, and reject it anyway.

The movie gets made, eventually. It sucks. Everybody knows they blew it, but nobody seems to care.

Down in the basement, Bob and the monster eat the dog food, then the dog, then the hapless dog-walker. Sated, they go home, and he returns to the word processor, whips up another saga, simply changes its name.

The monster, God knows, is still scary as fuck. And marketable, too. If they only knew how.

You really oughtta see it sometime.

S IS FOR SHARED TOP BILLING

When the aliens finally met with the things in the rafters, there was a lot of initial tension. Turf wars are never pretty. Much blood and fame were spilt.

But as it turns out, they had a lot in common. Ancient creatures with ancient bloodlines are bound to meet and commingle, every couple of eons or so.

A compromise was worked out. A sort of co-production deal. The fame-droozling worm-things kept the entertainment rights. The chitinous space-things claimed the minerals, slaves, and such.

All the other Elder Gods of Earth promptly folded,

under vastly superior firepower. Governments, nations, religions crumbled.

"WHO'S YOUR DADDY NOW?" the aliens asked.

And the human race said, "GAHHHH!"

But the fact was, the aliens *just weren't funny*. And the worm-things were masters of the human heart. They knew us better than we knew ourselves.

We have worms in our hearts.

And so it was decided.

We are governed by others, much larger than us. And we will never beat them. We are pets at best, possessions at worst. They will tell us what to do, and we will do something like it.

But that doesn't mean we're not worth entertaining.

You get better enslavement that way.

T IS FOR ME AND MY TV

My home is now in Sensurround.
I will not trade what I have found.
And I control all that I see
Forever.
Me and my TV.

There is no crowd.
I'm really loud.
You hate this flick?
Well, suck my dick.
I masturbate in privacy
Forever.
Me and my TV.

So now, in every living room,
We build our altar and our tomb.
United in our separation.
A different tool on every station.
Bamboozled by technology,
Still gaping at *Three's Company*...

As all alone as I can be
Forever.
Me and my TV.

U IS FOR UNRELEASABLE

There is no longer any such thing. Just because nobody sees it doesn't mean that it's not there.

Smaller worms—fame-free, oozing failure—are also a vital part of the ecosystem. They see to it that the unwatchable still shows up: on the internet, if not on DVD.

Rare indeed is the seeker, these days, who makes his or her mistakes in private. Why should they?

In this system of waste, everything still gets eaten.

Weirdly, sometimes shit tastes even better than Shinola.

V IS FOR VIAGRA

When Clive Barker made *Hellraiser*, back in 1987, the governing body of taste known as the MPAA forced him to cut one of his sex scenes for "too many consecutive buttock

78

thrusts." The number was three.

But since the advent of Viagra, the MPAA has massively slackened that restriction. Leading many to believe that members of the MPAA are now capable of more than three consecutive buttock thrusts.

It's a brave new world out there.

And believe me, we're not complaining.

W IS FOR WASHED-UP

You peaked at age 3, in a cereal commercial. They said you'd eat anything. The Audience smiled.

But the older you got, the more they never wanted to ever see your face again, as adorable morphed somehow right past normal to genuinely unpleasant.

It didn't matter how many eyeballs you ate, how much stolen skin you slapped over your own, how many times you tried to cut back in line. You were done. Living pathos, from that moment on.

Too bad you can barely remember your heyday.

Kids. They grow up so fast.

X IS FOR XXX

When you can't get paid to fuck in Hollywood, you know these are desperate times. Hippy-dippy '67 "Summer of Love" my ass. *This* is the free love.

Everyone's giving it away.

Used to be that pay-per-view softcore porn in hotel

rooms made more money than the rest of Hollywood combined. Average viewing time was roughly four minutes.

Thank God they're now offering snuff.

The average viewing time's roughly the same.

Y IS FOR YAWNING

They've been at it for seventeen hours, seven days in a row. Grueling, yes. But Yolanda learned early that there is one thing that you never *ever* do, especially in overtime. No matter who you are.

So when Wyatt starts to squinch his eyes, and his mouth rolls open, she swats him hard in the balls, hoping his yelp happens fast enough to cover.

But no, the yellow beam has already pegged his forehead; and the 1st A.D.—the director's right hand—has already turned, rage and panic in his eyes.

"Don't blow it," he hisses. "Don't you fucking dare. *We need you.*"

Yolanda, the script supervisor, pats Nolan Wyatt on the back and leans into his ear, saying, "You're the director. You're the leader. If you show how tired you are, you let them think it's okay to be as tired as *they* are."

"I know…" Wyatt moans. "I'm just…"

"Look," Yolanda says.

An extra has already followed his example. The yawning comes naturally. She couldn't fight it any more.

The yellow beam moves from Wyatt to the extra, turns red as it focuses on her head. The red helps conceal the spritz from the hole that blows open, kicks her back off her feet.

And nobody yawns for the rest of the shoot.

At $12,000 a minute, you just don't have time for that shit.

Z IS FOR ZZZZZZZZZZ

"So what did you think?" I ask, as we leave the theater. My date's eyes are glazed, but her mouth is open as we lockstep down the stairs.

"I don't know," she says. "It was kind of fun."

"Me, too," I say. And then she starts to slump and snore.

I wake up just in time to catch her, already falling in concert with her. We are in love. At least I think we are. And this movie argued persuasively that we were on the right track.

I feel the worms in my heart start to wriggle through ventricles, clearing out fat as they keep me alive. "I liked the car chase scene," I say, helping her up.

"The love scene was good," she says. "I believed it."

"Me, too."

"Good chemistry."

"So cute."

She teeters, snores some more.

I catch her even before she collapses, try to remember why I love her. A woman staggers past in a short black dress, and I try to remember why I want a piece of that.

Hypnosis is its own reward, and letting go is the heart of happiness. Given the choice between knowing and not knowing, the answer is so simple I don't even have to think.

We sleepwalk our way home, and through the rest of our lives.

The commercials are the loudest.

In our dreams, we are buying it all.

ZYGOTE NOTES ON THE IMMINENT BIRTH OF A FEATURE FILM AS YET UNFORMED

1.

I am dreaming a movie. What it is, I don't know. It will tell me when it's ready. Is already whispering to me now, unfurling itself like a softly windswept curtain.

The curtain is a place called Manitou Springs: a lovely little tourist town and art enclave at the foot of Colorado's grand Pike's Peak.

I am struck at once by the establishing shot through my windshield, eyes functioning as an imaginary camera lens. Capturing the colorful storefronts and sturdy Wild West architecture of its main drag, the scattered two-story homes winding up the green hills, the majestic mountain beyond.

The streets bustle with brisk tourist trade: roving packs of jocks and off-duty soldiers, clean-cut American vacationing families, delighted women on boutique shopping sprees, an impressive array of strolling lovers.

But the locals stand out, roughly 50/50 in the semi-dense sidewalk sweepstakes. They are shaggier, more relaxed and at home on these streets. Saying hi to one other, and walking their dogs. Most of them seem pretty happy to be here.

Beneath the surface, however, there is something deeper churning. I can feel it in my bones. Something special about here. Something exciting and strange, galvanizing every speck of sensation I have.

This town feels frankly full of ghosts, and older spirits from nature's weirdest depths, history repurposing itself for a 21st century America that, like me, knows far more than it understands.

I cruise leisurely through its heart in a cheap rental car, my shrunken stroke-addled dad riding shotgun at my side, curious pastel-blue eyes blindly unseeing, head cocked like a cocker spaniel's, a floating half-smile on his face.

"Oh, Dad," I say, over the car's cranked A/C, pushing the limits of his hearing aid. "Manitou Springs is knocking me out. Do you remember what it looks like?"

"Manitou Springs?" he says thoughtfully, every memory a struggle through fog. And as I proceed to describe it, building by building and mountain by mountain, he seems to go farther away. As if rekindling sight-based memory is transporting him elsewhere.

Not just through time, or space, but some other dimension altogether.

That is the wind that stirs the curtain.

2.

After dinner, I bring Dad back to his managed care home, where the slow death of hundreds of elderly bodies smells like Fabreze on old bones. The air inside is heavy with waiting and forgetfulness, but also with a kindness I can't help but respond to. It's so nice to know that honest human concern is at work here, at the end of the road.

We play a round of Yahtzee, and he kicks my ass. He can't see the dice, but he rolls them just fine. I don't have to cheat to declare him the victor. He is happy. That counts for a lot.

I help him make his way to the bathroom for his nightly prep, stand back for his private moments, spend those ten minutes looking at pictures of myself, my mom and sisters, his other late wife, all surrounding him, unseen yet comforting.

He comes out of the bathroom, strips naked and frail as I hand him his pajamas, help him put them on, lead him back to his favorite chair. The nurse comes in, gives him his meds. I say goodnight.

And drive directly to Manitou Springs.

3.

The Pikes Peak Inn is a cozy, inexpensive family-run joint at the mouth of Manitou's main drag. Two stories, twenty rooms. I am delighted to find an available room in tourist season, check into tiny #209, feel immediately at home.

Now the movie can begin to awaken.

I settle in, set up my toiletries and laptop, get out my note cards and medicinal weed. The residual dying energy still clings to my skin, but I need to be extra-sensitive now. Take the good with the bad. Take a toke. Feel it open me. Take another two quick, and done.

I punch up a concise Google search, give myself 15 minutes for homework before I start pounding the pavement. I skirt quickly through the tourist page, just to get my bearings, then beyond, garner several fun facts.

1) Manitou's rich abundance of mineral springs made it sacred ground for the Utes and other tribes, then a hub of health spas in the 1840s, as the town itself began to grow.

2) It is often now referred to as "the Hippie Mayberry" for its warm blend of high counterculture eccentricity and old-fashioned, down-home hospitality.

3) While Manitou evidently throws a mean zombie walk—with hundreds of its 5,000 citizens shambling up and down the square—its biggest weirdo annual event is the Emma Crawford Coffin Race and Parade.

This to-do is in gleeful celebration of the terrible day in 1929 when poor 18-year-old Emma—already 38 years dead of tuberculosis at the time—was washed down Red Mountain by torrential rains that unearthed her ill-buried coffin, and black-water-rafted her through the center of town.

I am really starting to like this place.

It's time to go explore.

Outside my door, the night air is cool and fresh, and I hear the soft burble of flowing water to my left. The carpeted second-floor veranda woodenly creaks beneath my feet as I come to a patio at the end of the railing: one bench, two chairs, and a low wooden table, overlooking the creek that runs directly below.

This water runs down from the mountains, and I can see in the tree-shaded streetlight dark that the long summer drought has taken its toll, the water level low but still powerful, comforting.

These mountains have secrets, and they flow through this town. I feel refreshed by them, spend a long meditative moment just soaking them in.

And listening hard.

In the parking lot, a car door closes. I see a nervous man in a ball cap and long sleeves, hefting a duffel bag and suitcase. He moves uncomfortably toward the stairs at my end of the building; and for the first time, I notice the blocky, artless police station just beyond.

I imagine his tense point of view, coming up the stairs, float a second imaginary Steadicam just behind him like a ghost. My own POV is the third camera angle, watching as he ascends into view.

"Howdy," I say, with an easy nod and smile to let him know it's all good. He nods tersely, eyes averted, ducks his face behind the brow and continues on, clearly wishing he were invisible.

I wonder what he's running from. Ex-wife. Ex-lover. Ex-boss. Ex-cronies. Cops. Criminals. Demons. God. Maybe just running from himself. Maybe all of the above. Maybe I'll just never know.

I center my gaze as a long shot, taking two slow gliding steps like a dolly sliding forward on its tracks.

He stops at #208, unlocks the door, and steps inside without a backward glance. I wonder what sort of sounds my next-door neighbor might make tonight, alone or otherwise. Hope for the best. Wish him no harm.

Then down the stairs, through the parking lot of strangers, and into the heart of town I go. My eyes are the camera.

I pretend I am that wannabe invisible man.

It's 10:00 on a Thursday night, and the sidewalks are almost empty. Nothing but darkened boutiques and colorful chatchka shops, a bookstore, a comic book store, lots of arts and crafts.

At this point, the only things open are bars and eateries that also double as bars. Music emanates from all of them: much of it live, almost all of it good. There's a sixteen-year-old white kid playing slide guitar and singing plantation blues like an eighty-year-old black man. I'm devastated by his old soul. Stop into the dive, like a hand-held camera, for a beer and a listen.

I want to talk with him, but suspect that everything he has to tell me is already in his songs. He is clearly possessed by ancient voices. I tip him a dollar, return his smile, head back into the night.

At the end of the strip—maybe eight blocks long, depending on how you count it—the hungry hungry hippies converge just beyond the Ancient Mariner, where the Grateful Dead's "Jack Straw" from Wichita is being earnestly rendered by a dreadlocked Filipino on twelve-string guitar. Evidently, it is Open Mic Nite.

I am old, dressed in black, and near-invisible again, so the young ones barely note me. I am not on their map. But out of the outskirts comes a ragged Charles Manson with glittery eyes and easily forty hard years of schizophrenic hustle behind them.

"Hey, man," he says. "You like movies?"

I laugh and say yes.

He brandishes a home-burned CD in an orange plastic case, the words BEYOND YOU BLIND FUCKERS scrawled in black magic marker. "Well, you ain't never seen nothing like this," he says. "This is the movie you've never imagined, telling you the things you've never been told."

"Then you've got my attention," I say, extending my hand. "What's your name, sir?"

"Scout," he says. "Cuz I been there and back. You wanna talk about the subatomic universe? You wanna talk about other planets? Other dimensions? Star-seeded data that precedes our creation, and lays the foundation for all that we touch, taste, feel, see, and smell, just for starters?"

"Don't mind if we do." And he shakes my hand.

"You got a cigarette?"

I hand him one, light one myself.

"There are emanations," he says, "coming off of these rocks that surround us. These mountains. This place. The fucking Garden of the Gods, man. Have you been there yet?"

"No, I haven't."

"Then you don't even know," he says, grinning one-upmanly. Playing the rube card. "It's not just CIA satellite crazy shit, Google spooks, or the Air Force Academy. It's not just Focus On The Family, and the 100,000 churches of Colorado Springs."

"That," I note, "is a lot of churches."

"This is the energy they're all trying to catch, but they're all too blind. Cuz they don't know, man. They don't know what really makes shit tick."

I exhale smoke, point at the CD in his hand. "So what'cha got there?" I ask.

His eyes narrow, as if showing too much bloodshot white would give it away.

"Twenty dollars," he says.

"I got a ten in my pocket."

He thinks a second. "I can do that," he says.

I pull out a ten, and we make the exchange. From there, he spends a couple minutes sketchily describing some amazing new technology he's developed, evidently able to read the waves between all things as never before.

Past that, it's a quick-slipping slope to sad self-aggrandizement, bitterly delivered by drunken rote. He's already made the sale, and sees no other prey, so now he's just dumping the load. How nobody understands him. How the world is all fools.

I offer to buy him a drink at the Ancient Mariner, and he defiantly informs me that he's been barred from drinking there. This doesn't surprise me a bit. I thank him, say good night. And he curls back into loneliness, at the outskirts of his town.

4.

Back in my room, undisturbed by invisible neighbors, I toke up and watch Scout's footage on the laptop. It's all just psychedelic fractal images. Patterns infinitely unfolding. Fascinating and stony. Incredibly colorful. But absolutely narrative-free. Not even a voice-over, or single chapter devoted to accusatory rants, which kind of surprises me.

The good news is, it's like tripping on acid with your eyes closed, so you can't escape the visions.

I like it very much, but have to admit I got more out of watching the creek.

Then I sleep, and dream, let the ingredients softly sift.

5.

And what I remember is this:

I am a dead and buried woman, coffin unearthed and slaloming down a mountain on a floodwater river of rain. The coffin is so full that the lid blows open, and I am thrust upright like a race car driver, whooping up gouts of rich mineral water that machine-guns from the skies as I careen straight through the center of town.

One hundred zombie walkers crowd Manitou Avenue, dodge to either side as I approach. Their green and red makeup runs down their chins in the deluge from above. Very much alive. Just having fun pretending. Playfully rehearsing for the end. And totally unprepared for this.

But I know dead, and envy them as I plow through their numbers, my eyeless eyes seeing them all too clearly as the red neon sign on the Royal Tavern comes roaring into view...

...and it's dry on the Royal's patio, as I hoist a beer to my lips, no longer careening. There's a skinny, lovely woman across the table from me. Is she dead? Is she me? Is she Emma? I'm not sure.

"Wanna know a secret?" she says.

"Well, yes," I say. "They're my favorite things."

She leans forward in confidence, sweet, spooky, and sly. Her white-blonde hair glows, backlit by the overhead light. Eye sockets cratered to black by shadow.

When she opens her mouth, there are no teeth inside it. Just a hole that grows larger, and sucks me in.

"Nothing," she says, "is very small, but very wide." Her smile stretches up over her cheeks. "Full of things we can't touch, and sounds we can't hear."

I take a swig, and all creation disappears.

"If you stumble into nothing," she continues, "you'll likely go blank, fall back out before you even know it happened."

I can no longer hear her, but I know just what she's saying.

"But when you're in it, you know what it is.*"*

6.

And then I am awake, at sunrise, remembering precisely that much and no more. Whatever other clues my unconscious may have dropped have skittered back to the dream-dark, where I hope to recapture them later.

Through the wall behind my head, I hear the invisible man crying, feel Manitou stitching itself into me like needles pulling thread, and suck up the twinges.

This is how the job is done: one puncturing, intimate little insight at a time.

My body is warm beneath the sheets, but the death-waft from Dad's nursing home still numbly rumbles in my bones. That energy is hard to shake off, at least for me, no matter how alive I feel.

Overflowing with forces beyond myself, I hop out of bed: just another little center of the universe, peering out through God's eyes, as I slip into the tiny bathroom and take a serious, much-needed morning dump of my own.

7.

Fifteen minutes later, I am driving through the Garden of the Gods. And oh, my goodness me.

Honest to all the gods there are, it's as if the angry red planet Mars hurled a massive handful of its coolest giant rock formations directly into space; and a million years later, they all somehow landed smack-dab in Colorado, at the foot of Pikes Peak.

It's insane, how profound it is.

Fuck Stonehenge. Fuck the Crystal Cathedral. Sheer 300-foot walls of majestic red sandstone jut unearthly from the heavily wooded Earth, as if to taunt us toward meaning. Some of them impossibly balanced on top of each other. Some splitting into uncanny twins like the stone equivalent of John Carpenter's *The Thing*.

Could a blind and indifferent universe actually stumble unaware into shit like this? How many trillion typewriting monkeys would it take to conceive of what I'm staring at right now?

I wonder about Scout's alleged technology. Is what he shot some actual readings from the rocks? Or is he just going all impressionistic, trying to digitally conjure some inkling of how this feels?

If there's one thing I know, it's that words don't do it justice. I instinctively think of where the camera should go. At pedestrian level. Vehicular drive-by's. A helicopter's God's-Eye view from above. Yawning ground-level views up their stunning expanses. Micro-close-ups of the fossilized textures themselves.

So old. So far beyond our recollection.
So utterly full of secrets.
I think it's time for breakfast now.

8.

Walking through Manitou in awakened daylight is a totally
different story. The bed and breakfasts are disgorging their
tourists. The locals are opening their shops, or walking their
dogs. Dozens of dogs, all relaxed behind their leashes. As if
this were the place that *All Dogs Go To Heaven* had in mind.

I find myself helplessly grinning, strapping imaginary
Steadicams to my knees in order to catch every canine smile.

I may be wrong, but it seems to me that these dogs are
somehow smarter than we are. Closer to their instincts.
More directly connected. Less abstract in their Gnostic
experience. More *here*.

And I think: if everything that exists is the center of the
universe—each thing experiencing itself from the inside, as
a representative manifestation of the greater whole—then
every perspective has innate and holy value.

Or at the very least, something to say.

I try to imagine every eye I see as a camera, seeing me
back and then beyond to something better. I pretend, once
again, that I am that invisible man from #208. Focus on
the not-me things that everyone else is seeing, till I'm not
in the picture at all.

The shot list is too huge to absorb, and yet I absorb
it, morsel by morsel. Brain shooting in Every-Cam, and
gobbling as much as I can.

A trio of teenagers walks up to me, unnoticing. And one of them says, "Patrick Stewart is the best Captain Kirk. No doubt." Am thrilled when they all agree.

Think *Christ, what an absurd universe.*

These jokes just write themselves.

Back in my eyes, just beyond the Royal Tavern, a courtyard opens up to the right. And from the corner of my soul/lens/vision, I spot a space ship, a racecar, an elephant and a pony. All vintage buck-for-a-quarter arcade rides for six-year-olds and younger, lacquer and plastic a-glisten in the suddenly painful sun poking out from a hole in the clouds above.

I take the right, wander down an alley-like promenade past dozens and dozens of rides, only to find it lined with room upon room packed with goofy games. Tracing the history of squandered time, in all of its funnest forms.

I was born in 1957, and can clearly remember the pinball machines of my 60s youth. How modern they seemed, next to the swear-to-God little-wooden-guys-running-around-a-baseball-diamond-if-I-hit-the-metal-ball-right-with-the-flipper entertainments I tried to wrangle at the age of six.

But here they all are, next to archaic Guess Your Weight and Test Your Strength devices that date back to the dawn of nickel slots. I'm guessing from the 1920s on.

When I hit the room jam-packed with Pac-Man and Asteroid, I am smack-dab absorbed by my own distant twentysomething milieu, with all the signature bells and whistles.

So when I see my 55-year-old self peering back like a ghost on Ms. Pac-Man's glass, I halt for a second. Trying to reconcile who I was with the reflection before me, like a color transparency in a high school biology textbook forty years in the past.

The reflection nails me. Throws me a wink.

And leaves me helplessly stuck inside the glass.

"You want a movie?" my no-longer-my-face says. "You wanna tell my story? I'm all yours. Have at it. GOOD LUCK!"

And with that, my body is gone, dancing out of my view, back toward the main drag without me.

Absent of body, I am a lens stuck on sticks, a tripod-bound static shot completely at the mercy of hands I no longer possess. Ms. Pac-Man races through the maze of my new insides, chased by faces with only one thing on their minds.

I want out of this maze.

The only way out is in.

I thrust myself out of the glass, into the circuitry, and through: coming out the other side of the device, and hurtling sub-atomically through air that feels like freedom and looks like a Steadicam running full speed. Weaving between toys and pedestrians alike, in one single moving shot that chases my happily rollicking body as it ambles down Manitou Ave.

I hit the stone wall of a corner t-shirt shop, find my consciousness plowing through the brick and mortar with no physical resistance whatsoever. It's like swimming through water without the need to stroke, paddle, or kick. Like I'm the tip of a laser beam.

I emerge in the shop's storefront window, catching up with my possessed bag of skin. It turns, sees me in its own reflection, and gives me a big thumbs up as it moves closer.

"WOOO HOOO!" it exclaims. "How'd you like that?"

I return the thumbs up.

"Now we're talkin'," it says.

And I am back in my own body.

"Try the European Café," mouths my reflection on the storefront window. "Right behind you. Do the Skillet Special, with two eggs, sautéed onions, mushrooms, peppers, and cheese on a bed of exquisitely seasoned olive oil home fries to die for. I'm not kidding."

"I love you," I say.

"Love you back," says the town.

And just let me point out: that fucking breakfast is superb.

9.

In summation, as I pack my bag and prepare to drive away:

Movies are creatures, with lives of their own. Just like everything else that is waiting to be born. If the right elements all manage to somehow come together, they happen.

If not, they were only dreams.

It's checkout time at the Pikes Peak Inn. I fly back to Los Angeles in a little less than three hours. Time enough to hug my dad, tell him I love him, schedule when next I'll be back.

His 90th birthday is coming up fast. An astonishing run, for one little life.

Time is funny like that.

Life is what happens when you're making other plans. And plans, at the least, are amplified best intentions.

I was a dream once. A dream of a boy my mother and father made happen. Who that boy might turn out to be, they had no idea. They just did it, then tried as hard as they knew how to make that little zygote wind up being somehow worthwhile.

Something they could love, and be proud of.

Something they were glad they did.

That's certainly how I feel about my own amazing daughters. And how I feel, right now, about this film about to be born.

I am dreaming a movie. What it is, I don't know. But I have sampled its ingredients, and tasted its essence. Can feel the puzzle box curtain unfurl.

Am inside that invisible man, who is running from something, and has wound up here. Where he will certainly be found. By what, I don't know.

Let's call it God without the beard and throne. The Fount of All Creation. The Source of All Secrets.

Whatever you wanna call it, I have found my Twin Peaks. A place of charm and mystery, light and dark, height and depth ringed by infinite breadth.

Not bad for a one-night stand.

I couldn't be happier with this tiny little room if I'd spent the whole night fucking inside it.

"See you soon," I say, pantheistically blowing it a kiss.

And close the door, till next time.

As the universe opens wide.

IN THE WAITING ROOM, TRADING DEATH STORIES

Okay. Funny story. So I'm walking my dog, Princess Balsac, so named because her face had more wrinkles than my scrotum. I don't know. Some kind of weird mutt mix. Like part boxer, part Shih Tzu, part gorilla? We never quite figured it out.

Anyway, it's our morning constitutional, about 5:40 ayem. My favorite part of the day, just walking and thinking, clearing my head for the chaos to come. Beating the crowd, as the fiery sun rises up over my beloved, embattled Los Angeles.

The Princess is sniffing around like crazy to either side of the road, ardently checking her pee mail. Yeah, exactly. My dad used it to call it "reading the morning paper," back when that was a thing. Lot of dogs in our neighborhood, leaving messages for each other, like graffiti for the underground railroad in the slavery days. This piss spritz means Rosco, or Pistol, or Dexter, or one of the local coyotes was here. And they went thataway.

At a certain point, I have to drag her forward or we'll never get done. If she needs to leave a message, that's one thing—on a practical level, pee and poop is what this journey's all about—but I've got shit to do myself, and you don't get much exercise from standing around.

So we go gallivanting down the street, serving as the neighborhood's snooze alarm, as house after house erupts with barking, groaning, and shouting, "Shut the fuck up, Clancy! JESUS!"

Just another morning in America.

There's a long sharp slope on Cazador, with houses on the left and a sheer drop on the right with a little island of grass and tree. This is one of Miss Balsac's favorite crapping zones, and she strains the leash to get up off the pavement and onto that favored ground. I laugh and run with her, hopping the double curb and trundling downward.

Halfway down the hill, there's a plastic Arrowhead water bottle one-quarter filled with something brown and hideous. Like a trucker bomb loaded down the driver's wrong flume, then carelessly lobbed out the window. It's been there for three months, and *nobody* wants to touch it. Except my Princess, who—like all dogs—is helplessly drawn to all things rancid.

"No, baby!" I say for the ninetieth time, yanking her close and away and just past, where she squats and disgorges. "Good girl!" I say, pulling the plastic bag from my back pocket.

And as I do this, I'm thinking about all the things we

don't wanna touch. Are afraid to touch, anymore, since the war came home.

I'm thinking about the Dairy Queen tragedy, just the week before, half a mile down the hill. A girl's softball team, loaded into one of their mom's SUVs, rolling over a paper bag stuffed with C4 and left in a pothole in the parking lot out back. They had come to celebrate their varsity triumph —Yankees vs. Patriots in a squeaker, 4-3—when their tire, then their engine, then their bodies exploded.

All dead. And for what? Some people said it was obviously random and psychotic. Anybody could have parked in that spot. Others thought it was anti-Dairy Queen or something, making a forceful and ugly statement about sugary treats, or the minimum wage. Still others maintained it was specifically targeted at female athletics: the new American version of Muslim extremists burning schools where little girls went to learn.

I'm thinking all this as I lean down to scoop up Princess Balsac's steaming softserve heap, mindfully doing my part to help keep the streets clean. It's like the least I can do.

We round the bend onto Falstaff, continuing down. There's a nice white elderly lady walking a nice white elderly poodle that yaps and strains at its leash, pointlessly wanting a piece of my pooch, even though my girl could snap its neck in a second. We humans steer our dogs to opposite sides of the street, exchange friendly good mornings, keeping pointless conflict at bay like the civilized people we are.

Barky and Jumpy are alerted by our approach, as usual, behind the fence that constrains them from the world: Barky barking by the gate in his coal-black coat, Jumpy running circles and leaping three feet in the air at every turn, like a Little Rascals mascot with a circle around one eye.

Princess Balsac is likewise whipped into a frenzy, and I wonder what they'd do if that fence ever came down. Would they tear each other open and apart, in brute savagery? Would they tussle and sniff each other out, assess some pecking order, show each other what's what? Would they relax, become friends? Odds are good we'll never know.

I yank her back from the fence, as Barky barks and Jumpy jumps.

We continue on.

And then I see the envelope.

It's just laying there, in the middle of the street. Padded. Gray. Its backside up. Whatever address it's aimed at is flush against the pavement, unreadable.

Princess Balsac and I approach, one step at a time. And with every step, I wonder more. It's way too early for UPS or FedEx, not to mention US mail. Best I can figure is that it got accidentally dropped, or maybe fell off the roof of a car driven by someone who forgot they put it there, got distracted, then got in and motored. Something I've done more than once.

There's a squirrel in a tree, and Princess charges toward it, off to the left. I'm pulled forward, forcibly yanking her back. We're less than three feet from the envelope, but she couldn't care less. "Fucking SQUIRREL!" is the whole of her universe.

I look at the envelope, now directly before me. Someone's message to someone. Thwarted pee mail. And I could help. Pick it up. Put it in the right person's mailbox.

I crouch, reaching down.

And suddenly, a terrible fear grips me: so hard, so strong, that I freeze in my tracks. Fingers inches away. It's so stupid, yet so clear. An instinctual feeling. Saying *no no no*.

A car is coming up the road. Princess Scrotum and I are in the way. Odds are good that this envelope will be run over. Probably something someone wanted.

I pick it up.

My arm explodes.

In the second that my hand vaporizes, my face catches fire and implodes, pushing my brain out the back of my head in a flaming spray: red, then black, then gone.

And here I am, with you.

So how is this a funny story? Well, it's fucking pointless, just for starters! I'll never even know whose side I died for. Could have been your side. Could have been mine.

So tell me: how and why did *you* die?

FOOD FIGHT

RUBYLYN

My name is Rubylyn Kole. I turned 30 years old today. And I'm so glad that you're coming to my party.

I'm in Female Seclusion. I have my own cell. I like that. I dance better naked that way.

I am dancing now, naked with my own shadow, watching her wriggle and writhe on the wall. My hips undulate. Hers elongate. My arms reach for the ceiling. Her arms actually touch it. My head whips from side to side, and snakes erupt from her scalp, flying free.

I am dancing to the music of the wind. Your voice. Its rhythms pulse through me, as the power of it mounts. I can feel you fill my body with vibrating particles of dust and sand, subatomic motion made flesh, can feel my moisture rising to the surface in response.

I am the feminine. You are the masculine. This is

foreplay. And it's totally making me wet. Soon I will be drowning in the sound we make together.

But for now, I flow, let my muscles loosen. Watch my black mirror's grasp exceed my reach.

I'm in Female Seclusion. But not for long.

This party's gonna blow the house down.

EMILY

My name is Dr. Emily James. I am 27 years old. I stand at 5 foot 3 in my business suit and sneakers, weigh 105. I am not a large person.

And I am kneeling in the middle of the sixth floor hallway at Golden Canyon Behavioral Health Center, watching its shit spiral out of control while the storm rages all around us.

On the floor beneath me is one of the guards. Her name is Kat, or so the others keep yelling as we desperately try to contain her. She's a *very* large woman, like an ape-man on angel dust, with the bloody key ring still jangling in her hand.

About ten feet to the left of me is the body of the last person she stabbed in the eyes. That was Dr. Carl Lily, the man who requested I be flown in here from L.A. at 5:00 this morning.

We had just been talking, three minutes ago, squeezing off the elevator with the female orderlies and their food carts, him nervously half-ass apologizing for the fact that the men had already been fed, so these were for the women's ward.

I said I understood about shifts and such, how you

couldn't do everything at once. I was trying to ease his awkward flirty geek nerves, make him feel less guilty for the innate sexist bias of hospital policy and his own surreptitious peeks at my cleavage, taking his apology and saying, hey, I'm pretty sure you didn't make the rules, don't worry about it.

But the sandstorm roar might have drowned out my words. I had a hard time hearing them myself. Unbelievable how loud it was, as we hit the main corridor, and the carts rolled off to the left.

Crisis Stabilization Ward F is split down the middle: men's ward on stage right, women's down the other harsh-lit path. There was a scrawny, high-strung administrator yelling into the phone at the nurse's station, but it didn't seem like anyone was listening. I wanted to say "Phones are probably down," but that seemed kind of obvious to everyone but her.

Except that no one else was around, in this otherwise-bustling hospital I'd spent the whole day ducking through the hallways of, veering out of the way of one crisis after another.

Dr. Carl looked at me quizzically, as if the same thought had just occurred.

And then from around the bend at the end of the men's corridor came shadows, draping like liquid across the floor. And I went, "Oh, no," even before the first human figures appeared, started racing toward us, casting long shadows of their own.

First one, then three, then eight, they came, like a football team chasing their own quarterback. Then the two in the back took down the one right in front of them. That was the first scream I heard.

From there, it all got louder and closer, till I realized that all of them were screaming something. It was all just blending into the howl of the wind.

Kat was in front. I saw her uniform, saw her mass, was strangely not reassured. The nearest people behind her wore uniforms, too. And they didn't look half as crazy as she did. They were just trying to catch up.

The first one who did yanked her left arm back, spinning her around. She stabbed him in the face so fast and hard that his legs kicked out from under him, shooting straight forward then down on his ass, while his eye socket squirted, and her arm pulled back, and he laid very still.

The next one pile-drove her a couple steps backwards, but was smaller, so momentum was all he had. They grappled for less than three seconds before she was snapping his neck, a chicken-kill move I felt rather than heard from seven yards away, and closing.

At that point, I felt Dr. Carl Lily step behind me. Not fleeing yet. Just cowering back, as I stood my ground. Grabbing my arm from behind.

I shook it off, and squared myself.

My name is Dr. Emily James. I specialize in para-abnormal psychology. Which is to say, psychosis so extreme that it takes on seemingly unearthly manifestations.

I do this for a living. It is not an easy job. Sometimes, things get extremely physical. Sometimes magick and madness are indistinguishable.

Either way, you cannot let them take you down.

In the last ten seconds before we connected, a male orderly threw himself at Kat's feet in full-on tackle mode.

She skirted him and smiled, plunging forward, jangling her bloody keys over her head like a trophy already won.

I looked in her eyes—you always look in their eyes—and saw the black vacuum I know so well.

She thought she would plow me over. I let her think that, petite sunflower that I am.

"RUN!" I said to Dr. Lily.

Then I went down low, palms to the floor, sweeping forward, feet first, and kicked in both of Kat's kneecaps, making them snap and buckle backward out the other side. She keeled and careened over me, shrieking, as I twirled and rolled out of the way. That should have been it.

Except Dr. Lily did not run.

She came down just close enough to snag him at the ankles, crawl forward up his body as he landed on his back, skull already concussing before she buried the keys in his left eye and twisted.

Only then did the others catch up. Drag her off him as he died.

And here we are now.

We've got her pinned on her belly. I am riding her back like a rodeo clown, knees in her armpits and hands in her hair, keeping her cheek pinned to the tile while people far larger than I am try to keep her from grappling free. It's taking three of us to hold her down, and I wonder how much longer we can do it.

"KAT! GODDAMIT! LET GO!" howls the black dude at my left. He's the one who tried to tackle her, now holding her arm down. And I can see his work boot is crushing the hand with the keys, grinding into the knuckles with his heel until they pop.

Her bloody fingers are still entangled with the key ring, but now it's cosmetic. They no longer work.

Still, I don't expect him to snap her elbow with his knee, then grab the keys and take off running back into the men's ward. I guess I should've seen that coming.

"JOE!" shrieks the orderly to my right. "WAIT FOR ME!"

Then he lets go of Kat's right arm, laughing.

"You're beautiful, baby," he says to me, and is gone.

Kat rears up on her last limb, and I dislocate her shoulder before she can buck me loose. Now she's the world's strongest quadriplegic, collapsing back to the floor and flopping around like an anguished crab.

I rise up from her, heart thudding, watch the two men disappear round the bend.

And all the while, the woman at the nurse's station stares at me, wide-eyed, babbling into the phone.

It's been less than three hours since they choppered me into this godforsaken Arizona hot spot, just in time to beat the sandstorm.

I still haven't met John Doe. Still am not clear as to my mission. But I have never seen a place more haunted by madness.

And now I'm wishing to God for reinforcements.

But that ain't gonna happen.

I am totally on my own.

WINNIE

My name is Winifred Sales. I am rolling a cart full of dinner trays down the corridor of the women's wing of Ward F. It is 6:00 PM. I am 46 years old. I have been working here for 16 years. Six plus six plus six.

I was 6 when my daddy left. 16 when my step-daddy first banged me. 26 when I got out of rehab, leaving a facility much like this.

This gets me up to double triple-sixes.

I don't know if that's why I got so drawn to the devil. It might be coincidence. It might be the numbers. I never really thought about the numbers much until I looked into the devil, and the evidence piled high.

Outside, I can hear him howling, feel the sand scrape against windows and walls, like fingernails trying to claw their way in. But he doesn't need to do that. He's already inside us.

I can hear him now, in every voice, from every room all up and down these echoing halls.

This may be his night. But he can't have me.

I'm on the Lord's payroll.

CHER

My name is Cheryl Kazepis. I am 22 years old. Go fuck yourself. They have me in the Female Seclusion Ward. Guess why.

I am staring at the slot in the door, where the food comes in. I don't need a clock to tell me what time it is. I don't need you.

The second she slips the tray in the slot, I'm gonna pull it in just enough to draw her hands forward. Then I'm gonna grab those hands, slap the tray out of the way, and pull her in here through that skinny little slot. I don't care how fat she is. I don't care how much meat gets squeezed off, rips away. Meat doesn't mean shit to me.

But she's coming in, bone by bone, vein by squirting vein. When the elbow snaps, I'll pull her in by her skin, undrape her like a stripper's titty when the bra slides free.

By then, he'll come and rescue me.

You don't even wanna know what we're gonna do to you.

PENNY

My name is Penelope Penix. I am 64 years old. That's spelled P-E-N-I-X. You say it like pen icks. That's how you're supposed to say it.

I wasn't born with that name. No. I chose it. When I married Pat. Before that, I was Penelope Pupe. That's P-U-P-E. You say it like yoop with a p in the front.

You're not supposed to laugh. It isn't nice. You aren't supposed to laugh at a person. A person can't help who they are. They're just, they're just people. They're just, I don't know what you want me to say.

Oh, the food's here. That's good. Yes, I'm hungry. Very much so. I'm going, I'm going to eat. I don't want to talk any more. I don't like talking. I don't like people watching me eat.

I don't like being seen.

JADE

My name is Jade, and fuck am I hungry. I don't care how

bad this meatloaf is, or what kind of bag these mashed potatoes came from. I just want this in my mouth right now. Ummmm-nmmmmm-nmmmmm. I am needin' this.

You really need to know how old I am? That's shit I don't even tell myself. I don't want to know. You don't want to know, either. Can I eat? Do you mind? I already told you my name.

Shut up. No, shut up. Ummmmm-nmmmmmmmm-nmmmmmmmm. I'm not even listening to you.

What am I gonna do when I get out? I'm gonna aim high this time. Find a train with some gravy on it. Little lettuce on the side. Make a meal out of life.

What? I can't hear you. The wind is howling.

I think it's howling my name.

WINNIE

My name is Miss Winnifred Sales, and four out of every five isn't such bad odds, considering. Even the crazy gotta eat. I don't have time to argue with bitches that barely deserve to live, much less try to coax survival skills out of people who didn't even want to in the first place.

We'll see who gets out of this alive. The Lord's the one wielding the scales. I'm rooting for some, couldn't care less about others, am hoping to God that the worst of them die die die die die.

I hope nobody steps between me and the end of the hallway.

I got someone to talk to down there.

LIZ

My name is Dr. Elizabeth Brody. I am 43 years old. I have to keep reminding myself that I am the skilled professional here. That my voice has authority. I've spent years. I've spent years.

But it's hard, because the wind is so loud now, the sandstorm like chalkboard fingernails across my inner ears, and the howling and screaming and loud restless chatter of the patients is wearing me down, wearing my nerves to a frazzle, even the staff in a panic, people not listening, nobody doing what they're told.

I keep trying to get ahold of Dr. Bromford, but he's not answering his phone, and his office was locked, and now Dr. Lily's dead, and some strange woman is babbling at me, and everything is horrible.

Everywhere I turn there's another emergency, but nobody seems to want my help. They look at me as if I'm useless, if they look at me at all, and I don't, I don't know what to do.

"I'M TRYING TO CALL!" I yell at the woman in the business suit and sneakers. And when she tries to take the phone, I bite her hand.

I don't remember what happens after that.

FRANKIE

My name is Francine Ogilvy. I am 36 years old. I stand 6 foot 3. And the next person who loses their shit in front of me, be they administrator, fruitcake, or whatever, is getting one right in the fucking teeth. I have had it up to here.

I am moving down the corridor, keys jangling at my hip, club in hand, banging on door after door after door and yelling "SHUT UP!" at the top of my lungs. They recoil if they know what's good for 'em. "Don't make me go in there and SHUT you up!"

Winnie and Meg are wheeling the dinner carts down the hall, and that's fine. I have no problem with them. They're doing their job. That's what they get paid for. I don't see them freaking out and flapping their little hands around like Dr. Brody, the dizziest dumbass dingbat this side of a padded cell. She's the liberal nightmare, all gutless compassion, with a backbone like a half-stick of butter in the sun.

This is the Crisis Stabilization Ward, for fuck's sake. I am here to stabilize.

And there's a part of me that can't wait till we get to the end of the hall, and Female Seclusion. That's where the action is. With the craziest of the crazy.

They better hope they don't piss me off.

SAGE

My name is Sage Rosewater Rainn. I am 23 years old. My parents were 50 when they had me. It was a miracle, they said. For my mother to be able to conceive, and then bring me to term, was karma meeting dharma like a charm, is how they told it, over and over, like a mythic New Age tale.

Then they both died, before I was 10.

And here I am, raised vegetarian, my face drenched in warm pulsing blood, gnawing through the soft meat of my left inner elbow. I tried the wrist, but it didn't grant much access. Too hard, too shallow to chew through.

But here in the crook of my arm, my plumbing comfortingly pops and sprays. I can cradle my face as I drink myself down, hose myself in the essence of life escaping.

Ever since I was born, all I wanted was to be gone. I never wanted this body. I never wanted this life.

As the tray pokes in through the door, already fading, I start to laugh.

"No, thanks," I say, through a mouthful of my own meat. "I'm already eating."

I hear someone laugh with me, behind me.

Only then do I become afraid.

MEG

My name is Meghan MacIlween. I am 51 years old, but you wouldn't know it. I lie about my age, my husband, my children, all grown, none of them who I say they are, and all of whom hate me. I lie about how much I enjoy my job, my co-workers. Sometimes it seems like I never stop lying.

I am telling the women in the sick ward that they need to eat, to keep up their strength. I am telling them this storm will blow over. I am telling them it will be okay.

Door after door, I serve them poison.

It was Winnie's idea.

I'm not lying about that.

I think it's a good idea. No good can come from the

voices I'm hearing, either from the wind or the pointless lost souls behind the doors whose last suppers I deliver.

When the last meal is served, I will eat one myself.

And if anybody asks, when my dying breath comes, I will say that I had no idea I was doing anything wrong.

CHER

My name is Go Fuck Yourself. And this is taking entirely too long. It's hard to sit still when your soul is erupting.

But the wheels are still a long way off. And the storm is strangely calming.

Save it up, he says. *Don't waste it. Let it build.*

I am coming, he says.

As I stare at the slot in the door.

JADE

My name was Francesca, I was 21 years old, and I never found out what my last name should have been.

In these last moments, I am floating above a dead hooker, fetally curled around her last gouts of vomit.

Then the wind breaks through the window, and carries me away.

PENNY

My name is Penelope. Penelope. It's such a pretty name.

How come I was never pretty?

Pat was a homely man. Pat Penix. Pat Penix. It wasn't funny when he died of lung cancer. But they laughed at his name. It wasn't nice. It wasn't nice, but they did it. Laughed at him. Laughed at me.

I just threw up again. I don't want you to see that.

Stop coming in the window at me.

EMILY

My name is Dr. Emily James. And from the men's half of Ward F, I feel a monstrous testosterone surge of mania flooding my way.

Standing at the nurse's station, in the corridor between, it had seemed almost balanced, the men and the women. Equally crazy. Equally overwhelming. Between Kat and the administrative scarecrow that bit me, I was even maybe thinking psycho women had the edge.

But now, with the phone in my unbleeding hand, and two useless women asquirm at my feet—cuz I decked that fucking scarecrow—I understand what Joe wanted the keys for.

Tonight, the madness is getting set free. And it's happening on every floor. Every phone line I connect to, at every level, has the same mayheminous story.

All are getting overrun.

Empathy is my specialty. That's how I do what I do. I feel what other people are feeling. I connect with them. And then I steer. I help them get from where they are to where they hope to be.

But there's nothing to connect to now, and what there is is way too much, too much for me, like trying to surf a psychic tsunami, a wave of irrational mentation so immense and intense that I feel overwhelmed, drowning in ever-mounting panic and madness.

When the first deranged patients start running toward me, casting their shadows, I drop the phone and flee to the women's wing, hoping to God that the men won't follow, haven't noticed me yet, won't see how horribly vulnerable I am.

I'm hoping they're going downstairs, heading for the front door, like a sane person would. Maybe heading for the mecca that is John Doe. The quiet eye of the sandstorm.

Oh, fuck, I whisper, as the pieces start to click in my head.

RUBYLYN

My name is Rubylyn Kole, and I am dancing. Dancing and dancing. As the shadows crawl up the walls.

There are ten of me, a hundred of me, five hundred and counting. Your rhythms propel us. Your voices are ours. Every one of us is different. And you know us all by name.

I undulate, serpentine, barely human at all. Every limb a snake. Every finger a tongue with teeth.

Today, I am born. Am born again.

Bring the walls down, baby.

Happy birthday to me.

FRANKIE

My name is Francine Ogilvy. And I am escorting Winnie
and Meg to the women's dorms, and the seclusion cells. I
see the door to the Matron's Office is open, was wondering
where the hell Madge was through all this.

Madge is at her desk, and all over the wall behind it.
I can't believe nobody heard that shot. Can't believe that
Madge would actually do that to herself.

Suddenly, the halls seem more dangerous than a second
ago.

Suddenly, I really want her gun.

WINNIE

My name is Winnie Sales. And when I see Madge, I go,
"Oh, my," and keep rolling. When Frankie doesn't follow, I
am fine with that. I don't know what she's gonna do when
she finds out what's really happening. Don't know which
side of the Lord she's gonna fall.

I pull up to the door of the first dorm, motion Meg down
the hall to the second. Each houses six women apiece, piled
up on their little bunk beds. They're the ones on Six with
the least to dread about them. The most harmless of the
deeply disturbed. I find I really like Karen and Lula, Macy
and her precious unborn child.

Is it a sin to spare them the horror to come? Is it not a
mercy and a blessing? I pray back in the face of the Devil's
wind, asking just that very question.

Oh Lord, I who art your humble servant begs to know:

is what I'm doing right or wrong? Especially with the whole Macy/baby thing.

At the end of the hall, it's another story. At the end of the hall, there is justice to be done.

I move to the door, with my prayer on my lips.

I feel a shadow move behind me.

The Lord behooves I turn.

Someone is running toward us, down the long length of hallway behind. The business suit throws me. It takes a moment to remember her from the elevator up. Cute little thing, talking to Dr. Lily, who couldn't stop staring at her goodies. Not from Golden Canyon. But shipped in from elsewhere, with security clearance and room to move.

She is running fast, like a thousand yard dash, past the sick ward and almost here, her shadow preceding her like a black carpet rolling out.

When Frankie steps back into the hall, she sees the shadow. She has a gun in her hand. And I find myself torn between hoping she shoots and hoping that this woman is some kind of angel.

"WHOA!" yells Frankie, as the woman skids to a halt, bead drawn at dead center. "Who the fuck are you?"

"I'm Dr. Emily James!" the woman yells back, reaching for the sky, wallet with a badge in one hand. "You don't know me! I just got here! I don't know you, either! HI!"

All the while, the wind is howling. Glass shatters. Walls shudder. Frankie squints at the badge as Dr. James moves closer.

"I just wanted to tell you that the men's ward blew open, and a swarm of crazy fuckers might be headed our way! So if we don't want to die, we might wanna find a room to hole up in! JUST SAYIN'!"

And in the time it takes Frankie to consider this, the first wild shadows hit the end of the corridor. I see them. Frankie sees them. Dr. Emily waggles her arms, as if to emphasize the obvious.

"IN HERE!" I yell, gesturing at the door before me. "We can barricade! COME ON!"

Dr. Emily waits for Frankie's nod. Then the two of them run up. I pull the cart back out of the way. "Open the door!" I yell, cuz Frankie has the keys. I can only pass the meals through the slot.

I see Karen and Lula at the window of the door, pressing against it as Frankie undoes the lock. There is blood on their faces and hands. She has to muscle them back as she enters, Dr. Emily close behind.

I wait till both are in before pushing my cart further down the hall. Don't wait to hear their objections. I am running out of time.

There is a slot that is waiting for me.

And the Lord says go.

LIZ

My name is Dr. Elizabeth Brody, and I am being dragged down the stairway by men who do not acknowledge me as a person, much less a person of authority, which I am, despite my broken nose and the fact that I am like a kite in their hands, an airborne puppet with dragging feet that bump off the stairs without volition, heading down and down and down toward John and whatever there is after that.

I try to tell them they should listen to me. They should listen to me. THEY SHOULD LISTEN TO ME.

But they don't, as I coast into the fifth floor riot. I'm not a person. I'm a flag that they drag. Waving it. Trampling it.

Breaking me apart, as I scream.

CHER

My name is Vengeance. And I hear you coming now.

There is nothing you can do that will save you.

Let's get it on.

EMILY

My name is Dr. Emily James. And I can't stop to appraise the horror until the door is totally secured.

I am pushing the beds up against the door as the windows shatter behind me. There are voices in my head. I knew there would be. Here they are. And they are powerful. They could fuck me up hard.

Through the window in the door, I see the men barreling toward us. Maybe a dozen. Maybe I'm optimistic. Okay, twenty. Twenty men.

Behind me, women are shrieking. Really bad things have gone down. I can't even stop to think how horrible that is until the first man hits the door, and I know he can't get in.

That man is Joe the orderly. His eyes are like a shark's, rolled back in bite-modality. The bloody keys jangle in his hands. His laughter is unhinged, off the hook, off the charts. He is laughing like a man for whom the whole damn world's gone funny.

When Frankie puts the barrel of her gun to the glass, he doesn't stop laughing. He just ducks out of the way.

When she fires through the glass, it's the next guy's head that blows wide open. When he falls, the next in line cringe back.

"HA HA HA!" goes Frankie, and I sigh with relief. So far, so good. I am glad that they're afraid of us.

Behind me, the women are eating the baby.

We'll take care of that in a minute.

RUBYLYN

My name is Legion. And now we are all dancing.

I can feel you. I am naked. Here you come.

John Doe. John Doe. John Doe.

You are everyone to me.

CHER

My name, my name, my name is Cher. Cher and Cher alike. You are not who I want. But you'll do just fine. Come on. Come on.

Through the slot I see you.

Come on come on come on. With the red keys, yes. In your uniform. Please.

Set me loose. You are coming down the hall. I don't care about the others. They are random. They are tools. They go off because they're stupid. They go off because they're lost.

They go off because they go off. Jibber jabber. Lost to me.

But you, Mr. Red Keys. Right this way! LET'S GO!

And you with the food? Oh, they'll be fucking you good now.

I bet we see that skin come off.

WINNIE

My name is Winnifred Sales, and I race past Meg at the door to Dorm Two, pushing my cart further down the hallway. She is paralyzed with fear, screaming "I DIDN'T DO ANYTHING!" as the mob advances toward us. The hallway is thick with bodies, the stink of masculine insanity, surging forward. It is the Devil's prayer, fulfilled.

And the strangest thing is, the stairs are directly to my left. And the elevator, for Christ's sakes. I could ditch the cart, and head down to whatever fresh hell might await me.

But there is no escaping this.

And I find myself thinking, if only I'd fed them forty minutes ago, we would not be having this problem…

…and then I start to laugh, running fast as I can. Not fast enough. But maybe that was God's plan.

I see the eyes through the slot, watching me. We may not get our moment. But this might be even better.

I screech to a halt at the end of the hall, just before the female seclusion doors, turn around just in time to see them swarm over Meg, her cart tipping over, food trays spraying all over the floor.

"FOOD FIGHT!" I yell. "WOOOO-HOOOO!!! FOOD FIGHT, MOTHERFUCKERS!"

The crazy men start laughing. I hoot again, start chanting, and they join me. "WOOOOO-HOOOO!!!" goes the echoing primal voice of the mad, unleashed. "FOOD FIGHT! FOOD FIGHT! FOOD FIGHT! FOOD FIGHT!"

There are three men on top of Meg. The one between her legs already has his pants down. But one of the others sees the meatloaf and mashed potatoes to his right, picks up the open tray, and smushes it in the face of Pants-Down Man.

"YEAH!!!" I holler, both God and the Devil in me now. "WHO WANTS A FACEFUL OF MEATLOAF, COCKSUCKERS?" I pick up a tray, peel it, hold it up like a pie. Prep another. "WHO WANTS A PIECE OF THIS?"

As it turns out, everybody wants some. Everybody not already all over Meg pile-drives my way, some of them pausing to scoop up her spillage, grabbing handfuls of crappy carbs and bogus protein, then slapping it violently, playfully in other people's faces or their own.

And I have to admit, as they descend upon me, that the end of the world is exactly as funny and stupid and sad and terrifying as I always knew it would be.

The first guy I hit in the face has a hole in his tongue where the stud used to be. I hope it makes the poison kick in faster. But he's an excellent sport, and takes a tray in either hand, then turns and pastes the next two sickos right in the kisser.

And everybody's laughing, including myself. I've got two more death-pies out, one in either hand.

Then Joe hits my cart, slams me back into cell door 03, and pins me against it, the trays flying out of my hands. I oof, grapple for another. He filches it from my hands.

Before I know it, my face is packed in dogmeat and gravy, lips tight as a virgin sphincter, every orifice clenched. I want to spit, but do not dare.

Then the cart pulls away, and he grabs me by the hair, slams my head against the cell door once, then twice. By the third time, the meat has fallen from my eyes, and I blearily see him, right up in my face.

"You're in my way," he says. And his eyes are the Devil's.

I peel some meat from my cheeks, stuff it into his mouth. Then I spit in his face.

"Hell's waitin'," I say. "Help yourself."

He throws me off to the side, keys jangling.

I hope he kisses her.

Then the others descend.

CHER

My name is Cheryl Lynne Kazepis. The red key clicks. The man comes in. I am kneeling like a supplicant kneels. Like a sucklicant. Which he wants. Oh, I know what he wants.

I take him by the junk and tear his nuts off at the sack, right through his pants. Bet he didn't see that coming. Had no idea how fast I could turn his sour grapes into wine.

He buckles. I chuckle, rising, plant one heel on his chin and feel his neck snap, crackle, pop. He is dead, and I have the keys. The red keys.

The door open. Me stepping outside.

Another man comes. I see him. He sees me. The things he sees me with explode in yoghurt curds that splish upon my wrists as one eye, then another eye unlocks with a twist of my hand.

A couple of the others are busy with you. They could use a nice distraction.

And I've got some bones to pick from you myself.

RUBYLYN

My name is Fuck and Undulation.

Won't you open the door for me?

EMILY

My name is Dr. Emily James, and I am staying put. Hanging onto sanity, as best I can.

The good news is, nobody's trying to get in here. Between the lock, the bunk bed, and the gun, we are holding steady.

The bad news is, they're eating the baby.

And there's no good way to look at this. This is the most horrible thing I've ever seen. Even the mother, her belly wide open, has a handful she's chewing as the light goes out of her eyes.

I didn't realize that Frankie was crying until the gun went off. Now I'm just amazed at how well she can aim through those tears.

And I wonder how many bullets are left, now that she's shot every other woman in the room.

She didn't waste the bullets, though. One shot per face, all of them fatal.

"You had to do that," I say. She isn't looking at me. She isn't looking at anything. But I say it loud enough that she flinches, blinks, shakes herself out of wherever she went.

Then she turns to me, and there's a moment where I'm not sure if she's going to fire. All I can do is aim my soul at her, look her straight in the eye, and let her know I'm here with her.

"I'm so sorry you had to," I say.

She starts to sag, then. I say, "Come here," and hold my arms out to her. She stumbles my way, wraps herself around me so hard it staggers me back against the bunk bed's frame.

And then both of us are sobbing, first her, then me, huddled close, while the chanting outside turns to a different kind of howling.

And she is so large, all around me.

And I am such a very small slip of a thing.

RUBYLYN

My name is Welcome. And as the door opens, in you come. I am a billboard of naked invitation. One, two, three of you. I don't care how many. Pull me down to the floor.

Every one of you is him now. And so am I. If we need extra holes, we'll make some.

It's my party. Everybody, come on in.

Let's make the shadows dance together.

MILLIE

My name is Millicent Marie Sales. And there is a moment, before I die, when silence falls, and it all slows down.

I can no longer feel what she's doing to me. I know it's

happening, but it no longer matters.

I feel something else. An enormous relief. I can't wait for it to be over. Then it is.

I no longer hear the wind. No numbers. No voices. No Lord. No Devil.

No nothing. Just gone.

As close to heaven as I will ever be.

CHER

My name is Freedom. My name is Victory. And everywhere, it smells like puke.

All up and down the hallway, it is vomiting men. Men, vomiting. Curling up in it and twitching. Crawling around in it. It makes me want to puke myself.

I do, get it over with, then look around urgently for someone left worth killing.

RUBYLYN

My name is Disappointment. All my lovers are dying. And the juices they disgorge are not at all the ones I'd hoped.

I think it's time to go downstairs. John is waiting. It's my birthday, for fuck's sake.

And I will be satisfied.

FRANKIE

My name is Francine Ogilvy. I am big and mean and ugly,

and I curse myself for that, every moment of every day.

But my God, you are the most beautiful creature that I have ever held. I can't believe you're letting me hold you. Letting me press myself against you.

Letting me cry like this. Letting me cry.

I have so much to cry about.

But your hair, your hair, it's so soft and fine. And your face is almost like a movie star's. My chin neatly rests on the crown of your head, and I can feel your heart beat against my belly as mine beats directly into your ear, between my breasts, so long untouched.

I squeeze you. You squeeze me back. I can't help that my hand is drawn to the small of your back. Down the length of your business suit. So tempted by the curve of your ass.

That's when I move in to kiss you.

That's when you make me feel bad.

EMILY

My name is Dr. Emily James, and I am incredibly calm. I understand this maneuver. Have been through it a trillion times.

"Okay. Hang on," I say, pulling back, looking Frankie squarely in the eyes. "Now here's the thing."

I feel her desire and pain, written plainly in her gaze. I smile at her because I feel her, and understand, and need for her to know that.

"What we have here is a grade-A insanity outbreak. We're not just dealing with individual crazy. It just passed critical mass.

"That means that we're all feeling it. All at once. We're in the Big Crazy now. Do you know what I'm saying?"

She doesn't. She is wearing dude's eyes. The eyes of desire. She tries to listen, but it all goes blah blah blah. She is watching my lips move, not hearing a word they say.

She moves in for a kiss. I squish my palm against her lips, push her face back. She doesn't like it, squeezes me tighter.

"Frankie!" I bark, taking her by the chin, high-beaming my soul-light straight into her eyes. "Snap the fuck out of it, lady!"

Her pupils constrict, her eyelids blink, raw lust and anger shocked into self-recognition. Her body, rumbling with danger, is caught in the act for this tiny split-second.

She could still hurt me right now. I'd have to kill her to stop her. If I could.

But I made her blink. And that's a start.

"Listen," I say, bringing one finger to her lips in a *shhhh*. "I'm here with you. I'm counting on you. And you can count on me.

"But here's the deal. You're giving in to the impulse, cuz this is all about impulse. That's what the insanity thrives on. That's how it gets us to give in."

She is listening now. Good. She remembers the gun in her hand. She remembers the baby. Hears the wind, and the death-rattle vomiting from the hall.

"If you give in, first you'll wanna fuck me. And then you'll wanna kill me. That's how it's gonna go.

"And because I don't want you to kill me right now—because I believe we can get out of this alive—I want you to pull your shit together. Remember where we are, okay?"

"Okay," she says, swallowing hard.

"We've got two choices. We can hole up here, and wait for these people to stop killing each other, and the storm to blow over. Or we can try to fight our way out, bring some order to chaos along the way."

"And probably die," she says, her sanity kicking back in.

"I agree."

"That would be stupid."

"Yep."

She lets out a deep, embarrassed sigh. "I'm sorry."

"It's okay…"

"But fuck, you're beautiful."

I laugh, hug her close. "Thank you."

She laughs as well.

A third laugh joins in, from the room behind us, making all the little hairs on my arms stand on end.

And that's when the bomb goes off.

CHER

My name is irrelevant. It will burn with my records. With no one left to care or see. Including me.

The naked dancing woman and I are the last ones standing when the fifth floor explodes beneath us, blowing us off our feet. We hit the slick tiles together as they erupt, flying up as we fall down.

The screaming from Dorm 2 is surprising and exciting. I hadn't realized there were still people in there. I'm not sure how solid the floor beneath me is, but at least I've got a target.

And the keys, still in my hands.

My shadow crawls ahead of me, drapes itself across the door. I rise to my feet, bring key to lock, throw it open, am killing even before I know who. Just another stupid woman whose name I'll never know. Then another. Then another after that. All through the billowing smoke.

Up ahead, at Dorm 1, a figure staggers out, promptly followed by another. All the while, the naked woman dances, back on her feet now and going to town.

All she wants is John Doe, John Doe. And I could kill her before she gets there. I could take her down right now. She is every slut I ever hated, every whore I ever had projected onto me, in false equivalency. Plus, she stinks.

On the other hand, she's my surrogate. She does all that fucking for me, so I don't have to. She's the vessel that's always open, the shameless wanton satisfier of needs.

She's my shadow. Or I am hers. She's my flip side. And I need her.

She's the one he idly bangs till he learns that I'm the one he needs most. The one who will stand at his side, and defend him against all comers, till the end.

I'm the one. I'm the #1.

Which leaves me with these other two. One of who's aiming a gun at my head, and going click click click on the trigger.

The other one squaring off before me.

So little and pretty.

Let's go.

EMILY

My name is Dr. Emily James, and the good news is, it looks like all the men up here are dead.

The bad news is, now I know where we stand on bullets. And if bombs are going off, hanging tight is no longer an option. I don't think the floor is gonna cave in, but I wouldn't swear on that.

We have nowhere to go but down.

Going back to the middle is out of the question. That's where the bomb went off, if smoke density is any indication. My guess is that shit is all caved in. We got off lucky, being off to the side, on the furthest wing. And it still fucked us up.

The only stairs left are behind the crazy-ass women before us.

And here comes one of them now.

Frankie steps in front of me, drops the gun and takes out her billy club. I fan out to the right, picking up the gun, just in case, as I clock our attacker. She is young, and entirely blood-covered. She survived all this. Is thriving. Has no fear.

"STAND DOWN!" Frankie yells, and the young woman shrieks out a war whoop, unstopping, weighing which way to land in flicker-flashes of eye movement that tell me she is not a berserker. Whatever move comes next, it will be calculated. She's that stone-cold kind of crazy.

I entirely relate.

"OVER HERE!" I scream. "YEAH!" Am I giving into madness? I honestly do not give a shit. Suddenly, I want to fight her more than anything in the world.

I am that kind of crazy, too.

When she veers toward me at the very last second, it's a quarterback move, and I am impressed. Frankie lumbers forward, too slow, out of reach. I brace myself for the coming collision.

And there, in her hand, are the same red keys. Aimed straight at my eyes. I imagine them punching in. Imagine my brain scrambling like eggs. Imagine her, in her moment of triumph.

I drop the gun, drop to a squat, pushing forward on the heels of my hands. Hope the floor holds steady.

Then I swing for her knees, and she leaps upon me, my feet barely grazing her shins, altering her trajectory just enough to throw her landing, my arms coming out from beneath me just enough to not be pinned as her weight crushes my back to the floor, shoulders taking the hit, my right hip hitting her right in the crotch.

She claws for my face with the keys, and I roll her sideways, throwing her balance. She stabs the tile an inch from my ear, catches my hair and yanks it as I slam her onto her back, both of us yelping, me rolling on top.

That's when I hear Frankie scream.

FRANKIE

My name is Francine Ogilvy. And I don't see her coming until she is already on me, jumping onto my back as I bend to pull that psycho cunt Kazepis off my beautiful girl.

I feel her mouth on my neck, like a vampire's kiss. And as I rear back to throw her, she drags her tongue to my ear, sucks my earlobe hard. My hands reach around, catch a handful of fine wet naked ass.

"I always wanted you," she moans in my ear.

I always wanted you is the echo in my head as she climbs around my shoulders, licks her way up my chin, then down. It's all I ever wanted to hear.

Then she tears out my throat with her teeth.

CHER

My name is You Don't Get To Kill Me, Bitch. As I claw at your face with my nails, rake it just below the cheekbone, leaving scars you will own till your dying day.

That day is now. I don't care that you just broke my nose, squirting blood in my eyes, squirting pain in my brain. My brain is made of fucking pain.

I can't stab your eyes, so I stab you in the kidneys. It doesn't pierce, but I bet it hurts like hell.

You scream. I scream back at you.

Then you punch me in the throat so hard I'll never scream again.

My next breath is impossible, and my sight goes white as my spinal column snaps just below the chin. I know I have a body, but it has been torn from me. Like a dream I can't awake from.

This is dying.

Holy shit.

But there is a voice in my head. It is his. And it says *you're still here. You will always be here. Forever and ever. Like an ache in the brain.*

You are the broken. And will always be broken. Forever wanting to be free.

Maybe next life, baby, his voice says, fading.

And if I could cry, I would.

EMILY

My name is Dr. Emily James. I am rolling on my back, off the dead woman below me, heart thudding from my scalp to the souls of my feet.

I am empathic. I cannot help but feel what others feel. I can feel her leaving, a black shadow forever draped on these walls, desperately clinging to their surfaces, for as long as they hold.

Frankie's dying, too. I am so sorry for that. I would have totally mercy-fucked her in a better, less unforgiving world.

So now it's down to me and the naked woman, who undulates before me, drenched in vomit and blood. Still sexy, in all of the wrongest ways.

She is debating whether to take me on or leave me to my fate. I'm feeling much the same way.

"If you're wondering," I say to her. "I don't want him. You can have him."

"Oh, good." She grins through bloody teeth, shakes her tits a little. "That means a lot. It's my birthday, you know."

"I didn't know that."

"Best party a girl ever had."

"Wow. Well, you have fun, then. Maybe I'll see you later."

"Thanks. I hope you do. Lotta cute boys down there. Sure you don't wanna come?"

"No, I'm good."

"Awww." She makes a pouty face. "But, ummm… could I have those keys, please?"

"You mean these ones?" Pointing at the dead girl's hand.

"Yep."

"Oh, I don't know," I say. "I kinda claimed 'em for myself."

"It would mean the world to me," she says.

I think about it for a second. I could kill her, or fuck it, just let her get herself done. It's her party. She can cry if she wants to.

"Aw, hell. Happy birthday," I say. Pry them loose. And toss them over.

"Oh, THANKS! You're the best!" she says, scooping them up. "You take care, now!"

"You, too," I say, and mean it.

Then she is dancing back down the hall, around the bodies, to the nearest stairway and gone.

I crawl over to Frankie, let her last blood gush across my chest as I snuggle in, hold her, try to let her know I care.

I try to be all the love in the universe. She hugs me back, for all she's worth. I hope the comfort carries over to the other side. Helps ground her in what matters. Takes her to another, better place.

And there she goes now.

As for me, I'm gonna pass on that party. I will wait here, hope the floor doesn't buckle. So far, so good.

When the storm ends, reinforcements will show. I'll tell 'em what happened. They will believe what they will.

I hate fucking jobs like this.

Good luck, naked lady.

Happy birthday to you.

RUBYLYN

My name is Rubylyn Kole. I turned 30 years old today. And the smoke is bad in the fifth floor stairwell, but it gets better by the fourth. Mostly dust and sand I dance through, watching my shadows crawl above, below, ahead and behind me. We look so fucking cool.

On the third floor, the stairwell is painted with blood, the walls more red than gray. The stairs are slick, with bodies all over, mostly teenagers and staff—oh those teeny tiny teens—and I dance around them carefully, bracing myself on the rails when I can.

By the second floor, I am hearing the voices. Still rippling with chaos, shocks of laughter and screams. But a conversational hummmm like a beehive is growing. Almost sociable. Like a party in progress.

I debate continuing downward through the body-stacked stairwell, or ducking in at the second floor landing. The door's right beside me, shadow fingers already draped across its knob.

A grand entrance down the middle would be twice as grand.

I grab the knob, and tally ho, on down the corridor I go. With the red keys a-jingle-jangle in my hand.

This was an open ward, so I'm not surprised by all the bodies. Everyone on everyone. You'd think there would be more. My shadows stretch ten, twenty, thirty yards. I find a discarded shard of bloody two-way mirror glass, and it feels good in my hand. But not another living soul.

I'm to the laundry room before I see my first ongoing rape. I bite his earlobe off as I slit his throat from behind, ask the furious woman beneath him if she would like to accompany me down to meet John Doe.

She says yes. And now there's two.

As we round the bend to the main stairwell, there are five women who are murdering men. I start applauding. They look up from their kills, see us coming. See our shadows cast upon them.

And then we are seven.

The staircase to the ground floor is lined with survivors who have not yet joined the churning mass below. On the ground floor, it is standing-room only. More than two hundred people, crowded before the front door.

Listening to the wailing of the wind.

Waiting for the freedom on the other side.

And here I am, with the red keys in my hand.

"LISTEN UP!" I scream, so loud that all heads turn toward me. *"I am the lock and key! I am the door, and the world outside, and everything you ever dreamed of being!"*

I dance down the stairs, with my women behind me. And they part, my people. They hear him speak through me. See my shadow cast upon one and all.

I enter the massive foyer, jangling the keys above my head in one hand. With the other, I drag the glass down my right side, opening a gash from ribcage to hipbone. Then I reach across to do the other side.

I hear the women behind me scream as the crowd falls upon them, know my moment is coming. Just two more quick holes to make, punching quick into my lungs, just above either nipple.

Now John Doe has all the holes he needs to fill me up, from every side.

As I drop, he enters me over and over, again and again. I drop the glass, but hang onto the keys, gasping for breath that will not come.

But he does, over and over and over, into my front, my back, my sides, every hole from bottom to top. He is in my ears, my nostrils, my eyes, the holes being carved in my feet and hands.

Meat on meat. Blood and jizz. Mind reduced to mindless frenzy, in the most primal dance there is.

It's a food fight, and we are the meals. That's all we've ever been. Walking tubes of consumption and nutrition, chowing down till it's time to give it up.

I give it all up to him now, and am gone, riding out on his voluptuous roaring laughter.

Best fucking party ever.

Happy birthday to me.

For Leza Cantoral

APPENDIX A

ROUGHLY ONE THOUSAND REASONS TO LOVE THE FUCK OUT OF ART (EVEN IF YOU HATE THE ONES WHO MADE IT)

I think a lot about the artists who inspire me. Those who've moved me in the past, or are actively doing so now. Think about what it means to me when somebody makes something that I totally fall in love with. A story. A song. A movie. A painting. A performance. An *anything* that has ever truly marked me. Changed the way I see and feel things. The way I think. The way I experience, and attempt to understand. (Not to mention the way I have fun!)

This is, I think, what communication is all about. And the function of creativity is to a) *find amazing things to express*, and b) *find amazing ways to express them*. In the process, figuring out who you are, what you love, what you hate, where you stand, what your aesthetic is, and how to somehow best put across that immenseness. Developing the skills that deliver the thrills.

So that other people might feel it, too. Whether they like it or not.

Whether they like *you* or not.

Cuz here's the thing: being a talented artist does not automatically make you a wonderful person, any more than being a wonderful person instantly makes you a talented artist. Most of us humans are a pretty mixed bag of good and bad impulses, daily struggling to sort that shit out. For quite a few genuinely gifted individuals, *they're lucky they're so damn gifted*, because otherwise nobody'd put up with their crazy-ass nonsense. And things like success and fame don't always bring out the best in people. Nor does the absence thereof.

BUT THE ART IS THE ART. And being a creative person is *not* the same thing as running for office, or sainthood, or even just applying for a job. For many people, including me, art is the process by which we attempt to cultivate and express the very best we have to offer, *whether we personally manage to live up to it or not.*

In many cases, in fact, we are drawing on our most personal, terrible, intimate flaws—and the even-more-massive flaws inherent in the universe at large—to try to make sense of it all. Sorting out the beauty and terror. The light and the dark. The potentially relevant from the merely distracting.

Just hoping to God, or the absence thereof, that anything we say or do has any meaning whatsoever. That honestly bearing witness—and *testifying to it*—counts as much for the sinner as it does for the saint. Recognizing that sometimes the most broken among us are the ones with the most profound things to say.

And, from there, that even the nastiest assholes among us—yes, I'm talking to YOU, Bill Cosby—have certain astounding components to their nature that make their art distinctive, and powerful, and true. No matter how betrayed we feel. No matter how horrible a person you may have actually turned out to be.

Doesn't make your transgressions remotely okay. Does not exonerate you in the slightest. But honestly? I only wish that all the truly beautiful things you did were not thrown up in some sort of attempted compensation for all the truly horrible things you were doing throughout. Because the good things you were doing were *so incredibly good* that nothing but a decades-long record of alleged serial rape, brought to light at last, could ever have taken you down. But down you go.

You fucking dope.

That said, most of the artists I know and love best are incredible people. Undoubtably complex and conflicted, yes. (That's the heart of the art.) Deeply feeling. Possibly difficult in life. *Definitely* passionate about their work. About life. About others. About what it all means. Committed to understanding as best they can. Then passing it on, so that you can, too.

These, to me, are all first-rate qualities.

So here, for your perusing pleasure, is a giant puzzle box packed with slightly over a thousand reigning members of my creative pantheon, spanning the gamut of invention.

Some insanely well-known. Some profoundly under-recognized. All working every angle under the sun and moon. Writers of fiction. Makers of movies. Highbrow painters. Underground cartoonists. Musicians and composers of every conceivable stripe. And on and on. You name it, we got it. (Even a couple of scientists and such, cuz that certainly counts as creativity, too.)

Some of them have been dead for a very long time. Some just showed up, are kicking my ass as we speak. A handful are so purely personal that no one outside my direct circle of friends will have any idea what I'm talking about. But most are, with a little research, liable to ring some sort of bell.

And while quite a few of them probably won't be winning any "Moral High Ground" awards in this lifetime, that doesn't mean they didn't change my way of seeing and being. As such, I have no choice but to thank them all profusely.

If you run into one you don't know, LOOK 'EM UP! That's what this whole game was designed for. To give you a sprawling glossary of my inspirations. My teachers, students, and peers.

Passing the torch is what it's all about, baby. From your hand to mine. And from my hand to yours.

Please feel free to make a crazy list of your own, okay?

I, for one, would love to see who made you.

***

Edward Abbey * Bud Abbott & Lou Costello * Anne Abrams * Douglas Adams * Neal Adams * Charles Addams * Cannonball Adderly * Adele * Hasil Adkins * Aerosmith * John Agar * Jim Agpalza * Robert Aickman * Joan Aiken * Alabama Shakes * Jay Alamares * Edward Albee * Doug Allen * Woody Allen * Adam Alexander * Leslie Sternbergh Alexander * Allman Brothers Band * Also * Robert Altman * Maria Amrhein * Laurie Anderson * Paul Thomas Anderson * Theresa Andersson * Kenneth Anger * Ann-Margret * Adam Ant * Danny Antonucci * Sergio Aragones * Gregg Araki * Roscoe "Fatty" Arbuckle * Arcade * Arcade Fire * Dario Argento * Rachel Arieff * Louie Armstrong * Darren Aronofsky * Lark O Arrowhead * Kayoko Asakura * Hal Ashby * Peter Atkins * Atoms for Peace * Lo Avenet-Bradley * Tex Avery * Axel the Jeweler * Hank Azaria * Tara-Nycole Azarian * The B-52s * Johann Sebastian Bach * Angelo Badalamente * Eryka Badu * Laura Lee Bahr * Chet Baker * George Baker * Josephine Baker * Rick Baker * Ralph Bakshi * Chas. Balun * Maria Bamford * Iain Banks * Banksy * David W. Barbee * Javier Bardem * Clive Barker * Barnes & Barnes * Peter Barnes * Roseanne Barr * Raoul Barre * Dave Barry * Bela Bartok * Count Basie * L. Frank Baum * Lamberto Bava * Mario Bava * Les Baxter * Amelia Beamer * Beastie Boys * Charles Beaumont * Ludwig Van Beethoven * Beck * Jeff Beck * Samantha Bee * Harry Belafonte * Adrian Belew * Amber Benson * Shaked Berenson * Leonard Bernstein * Beyonce * Bruce Bickford * Kathryn Bigelow * Antonia Bird * Brad Bird * Steven Bissette * Bjork * Jack Black * Karen Black * Lewis

Black * Black Sabbath * Algernon Blackwood * Thomas Blake * William Peter Blatty * Blind Faith * Robert Bloch * Francesca Lia Block * Lawrence Block * Frank Blocker * Neill Blomkamp * Mike Bloomfield * Don Bluth * Vaughn Bode * Peter Bogdanovich * The Bogmen * Eric Bogosian * Brian Bolland * Lisa Bonet * The Bothy Band * Rob Bottin * Loren Bouchard * Anthony Boucher * Darren Lynn Bousman * The Bowery Boys * David Bowie * Bow Wow Wow * Lombardo Boyar * Steven R. Boyett * Danny Boyle * Bruno Bozzetto * Leigh Brackett * Ray Bradbury * Scott Bradley & Peter Giglio * Hadas Brandi * Richard Brautigan * Jacques Brel * Joseph Payne Brennan * Leon Bridges * Matthew Bright * Caitlyn Brisbin * Poppy Z. Brite * Max Brooks * Mel Brooks * Mikita Brottman * Chester Brown * James Brown * M.K. Brown * Todd Browning * Dave Brubeck * Lenny Bruce * Bill Bruford * Alejandro Brugues * John Brunner * Brian Bubonic * Roy Buchanan * Buckethead * Jeff Buckley * Charles Bukowski * Luis Buñuel * Anthony Burgess * Jeff Burk * Carol Burnett * Charles Burnett * William S. Burroughs * Tim Burton * Steve Buscemi * Kate Bush * The Byrds * Nicholas Cage * James M. Cain * Cab Calloway * James Cameron * Donald Cammell * Ramsey Campbell * Truman Capote * Frank Capra * Captain Beefheart * Captain Beyond * Steve Carell * Timothy Carey * George Carlin * Wendy Carlos * Axelle Carolyn * John Carpenter * Brian Allen Carr * John Carradine * David Carradine * Lewis Carroll * LM Kit Carson * Brooks Carruthers * Angela Carter * Neko Case * Johnny Cash * John Cassavetes * Carlos Castaneda * Mort Castle * Adam-Troy Castro * Mae Catt * Nick Cave * Wyatt Cenac * Adam Cesare * Jackie Chan * Park Chan-

Wook * Raymond Chandler * Lon Chaney * Lon Chaney, Jr. * Charlie Chaplin * David Chappelle * David Chase * Paddy Chayefsky * Cheap Trick * Cheech & Chong * Stephen Chow * Benjamin Christensen * Autumn Christian * Robert Clampett * Bob Clark * Arthur C. Clarke * The Clash * Les Claypool * Patsy Cline * George Clinton * George Clooney * Henri-Georges Clouzot * Daniel Clowes * Christopher Coake * Joel and Ethan Coen * David X. Cohen * Leonard Cohen * Stephen Colbert * Kelly Cole * Mason James Cole * Nat King Cole * Joe Coleman * Ornette Coleman * Michael Sean Colin * John Collier * Bootsy Collins * Nancy A. Collins * John Coltrane * Jeffrey Combs * Francis Ford Coppola * Garrett Cook * Sam Cooke * Martha Coolidge * Alice Cooper * Basil Copper * Richard Corben * Roger Corman * Bill Cosby * Don Coscarelli * Rob Corddry * Elvis Costello * Country Joe and the Fish * Alex Cox * The Cramps * Reed Crandall * Wes Craven * Cream * Creative Underground Los Angeles * Creedence Clearwater Revival * Quentin Crisp * David Cronenberg * Crosby, Stills, Nash, and Young * David Cross * Tim Crowe * Julie Cruise * Robert Crumb * Justin Cruse * George Cukor * Dean Cundey * Rusty Cundieff * Chris Cunningham * The Cure * Alfonso Curon * Nicole Cushing * Peter Cushing * Cypress Hill * Cyriak * Rene Daalder * Ursula Dabrowsky * Willem Dafoe * Roald Dahl * Dicky Dale * Salvador Dali * Damage Control * Nick Damici * Steve Daniels * Joe Dante * Henry Darger * Bobby Darin * Bette Davis * Jack Davis * Miles Davis * Skeeter Davis * Dead Rose Symphony * Claude Debussy * The Decemberists * Deep Purple * Alex de la Iglesias * Paco de Lucia * Guy de Maupassant * Brian de Palma * Alex de

Renzy * Guillermo Del Toro * Graham Denman * Martin Denny * Ruggero Deodato * Robert Devereaux * Devo * Philip K. Dick * Ernest Dickerson * Bo Diddly * Die Antwood * Peter Dinklage * Steve Ditko * Divine * Dr. Demento * Thomas Dolby * Eric Dolphy * Fats Domino * Kevin L. Donihe * Donovan * The Doors * Gustave Dore * Eli Dorsey * Julie Doucet * Elissa Dowling * Kate Downer * Robert Downey * Robert Downey, Jr. * Sir Arthur Conan Doyle * Sarah Doyle * Heather Drain * Nick Drake * The Drifters * Mort Drucker * Daphne du Maurier * Caroline du Potet * Mike Dubisch * George Duke * Katherine Dunn * George Dunning * Lord Dunsany * Bob Dylan * Clint Eastwood * Roger Ebert * Arantxa Echevarria * Blake Edwards * Electric Light Orchestra * Danny Elfman * Richard Elfman * Duke Ellington * Harlan Ellison * Ralph Ellison * Emerson, Lake, and Palmer * Brian Emrich * Victoria English * Brian Eno * En Vogue * M.C. Escher * Esquivel * Dennis Etchison * Patrick Ewald * Gareth Evans * The Everly Brothers * Brad Falchuk * Todd Farmer * Bobby & Peter Farrelly * John Farris * Mia Farrow * William Faulkner * Louisa Feldman * Al Feldstein * Federico Fellini * Mike Figgis * David Fincher * Fine Young Cannibals * Jack Finney * The Firesign Theater * Peter Fischli & David Weiss * Terence Fisher * Fitz and the Tantrums * Flaming Lips * Bela Fleck * Mary Fleener * Fleetwood Mac * Max & Dave Fleischer * Florence + The Machine * The Flying Saucers * James Foley * Milos Forman * Jim Fortier * Bruno Forzani & Helene Cattet * Bob Fosse * The Four Tops * Aretha Franklin * Carl Franklin * Franz Ferdinand and Sparks * Frank Frazetta * Dana Fredsti * Robert Fripp * Bill Frisell * Dwight Frye *

Robert Fuest * Kinji Fukasaku * Lucio Fulci * Buckminster Fuller * Samuel Fuller * Peter Gabriel * Neil Gaiman * Serge Gainsborg * Vikram Gandhi * John Gardner * Garfunkel & Oates * Alex Garland * Dick Gregory * Adam Gierasch & Jace Anderson * William Gay * Marvin Gaye * George Gershwin * Gentle Giant * William Gibson * H.R. Giger * Terry Gilliam * Vince Gilligan * Karen Gillan * Dizzy Gillespie * Jonathan Glazer * Jackie Gleason * Phoebe Glockner * Crispin Glover * Goblin * Drew Goddard * Martha Goddard * Adam Golaski * Rube Goldberg * Andrew Goldfarb * William Golding * William Goldman * Diane Ayala Goldner * Jerry Goldsmith * Bobcat Goldthwait * Michel Gondry * Cody Goodfellow * Benny Goodman * Archie Goodwin * The Goon Show * Ruth Gordon * Stuart Gordon * Edward Gorey * Gorillaz * John Gorumba * Jessie Gotta * Gilbert Gottfried * Gotye * Dana Gould * Danis Goulet * Matthew Granberry * Michael Granberry * Grand Funk Railroad * Richard E. Grant * Stephane Grappelli * The Grateful Dead * Tessa Gratton * David Gray * Devora Gray * Adam Green * Al Green * Justin Green * Peter Greenaway * John Greyson * Angela Grillo * Charles B. Griffith * Grizzly Bear * Matt Groening * Stanislav Grof * Richard Grove * Tony Grow * Davis Grubb * Nick Gucker * Gigi Saul Guerrero * Christopher Guest * Guns N' Roses * James Gunn * Trent Haaga * Nina Hagen * Merle Haggard * Stacy Pippi Hammon * Paula Rozelle Hanback * Mykle Hansen * Billy Hanson * Harman & Ising * Dan Harmon * Curtis Harrington * Danielle Harris * Emmylou Harris * Kathyjean Harris * Thomas Harris * Ray Harryhausen * Veronica Hart * Phil Hartman * Herke Harvey * P.J. Harvey * Rhondo Hatton * John

Hawkes * Coleman Hawkins * Screaming Jay Hawkins * Howard Hawks * Kiralee Hayashi * Todd Haynes * Glenn Head * Heart * Robert Heinlein * Joseph Heller * Ed Helms * Tony Hendra * Jimi Hendrix * Frank Henenlotter * Jim Henson * Audrey Hepburn * Frank Herbert * Bernard Hermann * Gilberto y Jaime Hernandez * Werner Herzog * Bill Hicks * Dan Hicks & His Hot Licks * Colin Higgins * George Roy Hill * Jack Hill * Walter Hill * Alfred Hitchcock * Robyn Hitchcock * Brian Hodge * John Hodgman * Brad C. Hodson * Philip Seymour Hoffman * Billie Holiday * Tom Holland * Judy Holliday * The Hollies * Buddy Holly * Matthew Currie Holmes * Rand Holmes * Gustav Holst * Seth Holt * Heidi Honeycutt * John Lee Hooker * Jesca Hoop * Tobe Hooper * Lightnin' Hopkins * Dennis Hopper * Robert E. Howard * Del & Sue Howison * Howlin' Wolf * Tim Hunter * Zora Neale Hurston * John Hurt * Mississippi John Hurt * Aldous Huxley * John Hyams * Ice Cube * Ice T * Billy Idol * Interpol * INXS * Eugene Ionesco * Greg Irons * Margaret Irwin * Katsuhito Ishii * Hajime Ishimine * Juzo Itami * It's A Beautiful Day * It's Always Sunny in Philadelphia * Ub Iwerks * Eddie Izzard * Mahalia Jackson * Peter Jackson * Shirley Jackson * Emma Jacobs * Al Jaffee * Etta James * The James Gang * Jim Jarmusch * Zak Jarvis * Jaxon (Jack Edward Jackson) * Timothy Leary * Jefferson Airplane * Jethro Tull * Joan Jett * Jean-Pierre Jeunet * Antonio Carlos Jobim * Alejandro Jodorowsky * Angelina Jolie * Elton John * George Clayton Johnson * Jeremy Robert Johnson * Tor Johnson * George Jones * Jason Jones * Norah Jones * Spike Jones * Tom Jones * Spike Jonez * Janis Joplin * Scott Joplin * Rhoda Jordan * Mike Judge * Carl Jung *

Franz Kafka * Boris Karloff * Andrew Kasch * Charlie Kaufman * Lloyd Kaufman * Philip Kaufman * Kaz * Michael Kazepis * Margaret Keane * Buster Keaton * Michael Keaton * Brian Keene * Walt Kelly * Jennifer Kent * Doug Kershaw * Ken Kesey * Jack Ketchum * Key & Peele * Daniel Keyes * Nusrat Fateh Ali Khan * The Kids In the Hall * B.B. King * Carole King * Stephen King * King Crimson * The Kinks * Klaus Kinski * Jack Kirby * Abdul Mati Klarwein * T.E.D. Klein * Jordan Klepper * B. Kliban * Daniel Knauf * KNB * Jenji Kohan * Kathe Koja * Alethea Kontis * Harmony Korine * Ernie Kovacs * Jan Kozlowski * Jon Kricfalusi * Kris Kristofferson * Kristine Kryttre * Stanley Kubrick * Akira Kurosawa * Ed Kurtz * Tony Kushner * Harvey Kurtzman * Karen Lam * John Landis * Roberta Lannes * Fritz Lang * kd lang * Sarah Langan * Joe R. Lansdale * Shannon Lark & Lori Bowen * Gary Larson * Bill Laswell * Charles Laughton * Tom Laughlin * Pascal Laugier * Cyndi Lauper * Carol Lay * Mark Lazzo * Leadbelly * Led Zeppelin * Christopher Lee * Izzy Lee * Peggy Lee * Spike Lee * Tanith Lee * Tom Lehrer * Jennifer Jason Leigh * Jack Lemmon * John Lennon * Annie Lennox * Elmore Leonard * Sergio Leone * Ira Levin * Marc Levinthal * Violet LeVoit * Val Lewton * Garrett Liggett * Lil Sum'n Sum'n * Bentley Little * Little Richard * Nadia Litz * Livia Llewelyn * Harold Lloyd * Julie London * Frank Belknap Long * Ben Loory * Lorde * Kerr Lordygan * Jan-Michael Losada * Joseph Losey * Courtney Love * H.P. Lovecraft * Lene Lovich * The Lovin' Spoonful * Emmanual Lubezki * Tim Lucas * Clare Boothe Luce * Sidney Lumet * Ida Lupino * John Lydon * David Lynch * Jennifer Lynch * Joe Lynch * Adrian Lyne * Loretta Lynn *

Philip MacDonald * Seth MacFarlane * Shirley MacLaine * William H. Macy * Guy Maddin * Madness * Al Madrigal * Ann Magnuson * Rene Magritte * Taj Mahal * Mahavishnu Orchestra * Matt Maiellaro * Malaclypse the Younger * Josh Malerman * Nick Mamatas * David Mamet * Henry Mancini * Aasif Mandvi * Aimee Mann * Clint Mansell * Marilyn Manson * Greil Marcus * Bob Marley * Jay Marshall * Neil Marshall * Don Martin * Steve Martin * The Marx Brothers * Elizabeth Massie * Massive Attack * Chris Matheson & Ed Solomon * Richard Matheson * Richard Christian Matheson * Paul Mavrides * John Mayall * Carol McArthur * Simon McCaffery * Robert R. McCammon * Kimberly McCollough * Ian McDowell * Rose McGowan * Micheal McKean * Lucky McKee * Rebekah & David McKendry * Chase McKenna * Terence McKenna * Shane McKenzie * John McNaughton * Peter Medak * Joe Meek * Fernando Meirelles * George Melies * Carlton Mellick III * Mike Mendez * Andy Merrill * Trista Metz * Radley Metzger * Richard Metzger * Russ Meyer * Lorne Michaels * Peter Rida Michail * Toshiro Mifune * Takeshi Miike * Shunichiro Miki * David Milch * John Milius * Chris Miller * Dick Miller * George Miller * Vinciane Millereau * Tony Millionaire * Hasan Minhaj * David Robert Mitchell * Duke Mitchell * John Cameron Mitchell * Joni Mitchell * Robert Mitchum * Hayao Miyazaki * Moloko Plus * The Monkees * Monty Python's Flying Circus * The Moody Blues * Alan Moore * Andrew Moore * Julianne Moore * Rudy Ray Moore * Terry & Christopher Morgan * Morphine * Ennio Morricone * Gray Morrow * Jelly Roll Morton * Lisa Morton * Jenn Moss * Mountain * Phil Mucci * Martin Mull * Robby

Muller * Mumbo's Brain * Peter Murphy * Bob Murawski * Walter Murch * Ryan Murphy * Bill Murray * Muse * Justine Musk * Modest Mussorgsky * Mystery Science Theater 3000 * Hideo Nakata * Napoleon XIV * Nash the Slash * Yvonne Navarro * Brad Neely * Willie Nelson * Mark Newgarden * Paul Newman * Bree Newsome * Mike Nichols * Jack Nicholson * Gregory Nicoll * Greg Nicotero * Nirvana * William F. Nolan * Philip Nutman * NWA * Joyce Carol Oates * Warren Oates * Dan O'Bannon * Richard O'Brien * Weston Ochse * Flannery O'Conner * Bob Odenkirk * Michael O'Donohue * Rose O'Keefe * Chloe Okuno * Gary Oldman * Jon Oliver * Larry O'Neil * The Onion * Roy Orbison * Orbital * George Orwell * J. David Osborne * Nagisa Oshima * Patton Oswalt * Katsuhiro Otomo * Peter O'Toole * Outkast * Michael Ouweleen & Erik Richter * Rick Overton * Frank Oz * Damon Packard * Chuck Palahniuk * Amanda Palmer * Gary Panter * Dennis Paoli * Nick Park * Alan Parker * Charlie Parker * Dave Parker * Dorothy Parker * Robert Parker * Trey Parker & Matt Stone * Gordon Parks * Michael Parks * Maxfield Parrish * Dolly Parton * Norman Partridge * Jaco Pastorius * Mike Patton * Les Paul * Bill Paxton * PCO * Anthony Pearce * Pearl Jam * Sam Peckinpah * Simon Pegg * Harvey Pekar * Penn & Teller * Lindsey Peterson * Tom Piccirilli * Wilson Pickett * Cameron Pierce * Kirsten Alene Pierce * Charles Pinion * Pink * Pink Floyd * Robert Pirigi * Brad Pitt * Pixar * The Pixies * Plotz * The Plugz * Amanda Plummer * Bill Plympton * Edgar Allan Poe * Sidney Poitier * Chris Poland * Roman Polanski * Tim Polecat * The Police * Iggy Pop * Portishead * Parker Posey * Postal Service * Count Jan

Potocki * Dennis Potter * Michael Powell * Perez Prado *
Terry Pratchett * Elvis Presley * The Pretenders * Vincent
Price * Prince * John Prine * Emily Procter * Richard Pryor
* Jackson Publick * Puddles Pity Party * Tito Puente *
Thomas Pynchon * Dennis Quaid * Randy Quaid * The
Brothers Quay * Queen * Queens of the Stone Age *
Radiohead * Rage Against the Machine * Sam Raimi *
RATATAT * Readership Hostile * Red Hot Chili Peppers *
Otis Redding * Adam Reed * Carol Reed * Oliver Reed *
Martha Reeves and the Vandelles * Michael Reeves *
Wilhem Reich * John C. Reilly * Django Reinhardt *
R.E.M. * The Residents * Paul Reubens * Matthew Revert
* Trent Reznor * Luke Rhinehart * Buddy Rich * Robert
Richardson * Nelson Riddle * Diana Rigg * The Righteous
Brothers * Marty Robbins * Tom Robbins * Bruce Robinson
* Robbie Robertson * The Roches * Chris Rock * Gene
Roddenberry * Jimmie Rodgers * Rodrigo y Gabriela *
Robert Rodriguez * Nicholas Roeg * Seth Rogen * The
Rolling Stones * Henry Rollins * Sonny Rollins * Mark
Romanek * George A. Romero * Daniel Rosenboom *
Diana Ross and The Supremes * Robert Rossen * Nino
Rota * Big Daddy Roth * David Lee Roth * Roxy Music *
Joseph Ruben * Bruce Joel Rubin * Todd Rundgren * Lou
Rusconi * J.S. Russell * Ken Russell * Leon Russell * Ray
Russell * Rosalind Russell * Mark Ryden * Saki * Sam the
Sham and the Pharaohs * Bradley Sands * Jimmy Sangster
* William Sansom * Santana (original band) * George
Saunders * Savages * Tom Savini * Savoy Brown * Stephen
Sayadian * John Sayles * Tiffany Scandal * Kristen Schaal *
Lalo Schifrin * Ryan Schifrin * David Schmoeller * David
J. Schow * Budd Schulberg * Amy Schumer * Martin

Scorsese * George C. Scott * Noel Jason Scott * Raymond Scott * Ridley Scott * Tony Scott * Alexander Scriabin * Alisha Seaton * Secret Chiefs 3 * Dori Seda * Amy Sedaris * David Sedaris * Peter Sellers * Rod Serling * Dr. Seuss * Tyrrell Shaffner * William Shakespeare * Eric Shapiro * Michael Shea * Robert Shea * Harry Shearer * Mary Shelley * Allan Sherman * Kate Shenton * The Shirelles * John Shirley * Wayne Shorter * Mark Shostrom * Shpongle * Don Siegal * Bob Sikoryak * Sarah Silverman * Simon and Garfunkel * Nina Simone * Simple Minds * Nancy Sinatra * Siouxsie and the Banshees * Tom Six * Graham Skipper * Danger Slater * Henry Slesar * Jimmy Slonina * Sly and the Family Stone * Brendon Small * Clark Ashton Smith * Dick Smith * Kevin Smith * The Smiths * Michele Soavi * Steven Soderbergh * Paul Solet * Jay Sommers * Soundgarden * Stephen Sondheim * Jen and Sylvia Soska * Soul Coughing * Terry Southern * Craig Spector * Art Spiegelman * The Spinners * Norman Spinrad * Spirit * Bruce Springsteen * Dan Spurgeon * Carl Stalling * Dino Stamatopoulos * Rev. Ivan Stang * Krawczyk Stanislav * Harry Dean Stanton * Barbara Stanwyck * Ray Dennis Steckler * Ralph Steadman * Barbara Steele * James Steele * Steely Dan * Joseph Stefano * Count Eric Stanislaus Stenbock * Steppenwolf * Jim Steranko * Tom Stern * Cat Stevens * Dave Stevens * Carl Stephenson * Jon Stewart * Bram Stoker * Oliver Stone * William Stout * Peter Straub * Meryl Streep * Theodore Sturgeon * Preston Sturges * St. Vincent * Yma Sumac * Supertramp * Donald Sutherland * Kiefer Sutherland * Tammi Sutton * Jan Svankmajer * Jonathan Swift * Tilda Swinton * T. Rex. * Talking Heads * Tangerine Dream * Quentin Tarantino * Mara Gasparro

Tasker * Art Tatum * Bernie Taupin * Julie Taymore * Pyoter Illyich Tchaikovsky * Lewis Teague * Tears For Fears * Melanie Tem * Steve Rasnic Tem * Temple of the Dog * Gavin Templeton * The Temptations * Ten Years After * John Terlazzo * Sonny Terry & Brownie McGhee * Nikola Tesla * Walter Tevis * Thee Oh Sees * Thin Lizzy * Jim Thirwell * Donna Thorland & Peter Podgursky * The Three Stooges * The Three Suns * Hunter S. Thompson * Jim Thompson * Rebecca Thomson * Billy Bob Thorton * James Thurber * Jen Thym * James Toback * Amon Tobin * J.R.R. Tolkien * Michael Tolkin * Lily Tomlin * Isao Tomita * Roy Tompkins * Tonio K. * Tool * Robert Towne * Traffic * Treat Her Right * Robin Trower * G. B. Trudeau * Douglas Trumbull * Helen Truong * The Tubes * McCoy Tyner * Susan Tyrrell * U2 * UB40 * Edgar G. Ulmer * Ultimate Spinach * Ian Underwood * Ruth Underwood * Unknown Hinson * Steve Vai * Edgar Varese * Glen Vasey * Brian K. Vaughan * Sarah Vaughan * Stevie Ray Vaughan * Conrad Veidt * The Velvet Underground * Villagers * Athena Villaverde * Will Vinton * Kayley Viteo * Kurt Vonnegut, Jr. * MS Waddell * Karl Edward Wagner * Tom Waits * Chris Walas * Christopher Walken * T-Bone Walker * Amy Wallace * Eli Wallach * Fats Waller * Buz Danger Wallick * Julia Walter * Pat Walter * Stephen Walter * Wang Chung * Jay Ward * M. Ward * Dan Waters * John Waters * Muddy Waters * Roger Watkins * Bill Watterson * Alan Watts * Weather Report * Ween * Peter Weller * Orson Welles * Jen Wenger * Nathanael West * Donald Westlake * Peter Weir * H.G. Wells * Haskell Wexler * Jen Wexler * James Whale * Sean Whalen * Joss Whedon * Jack White * Mack White * Slim Whitman * The Who * Robert Wiele *

Barbie Wilde * Billy Wilder * Leslianne Wilder * Fred Willard * Caroline Williams * Hank Williams III * Hank Williams, Sr. * Jessica Williams * J.R. Williams * Paul Williams * Richard Williams * Robt. Williams * Robin Williams * Al Williamson * Sonny Boy Williamson * Dave Willis * Bob Wills & His Texas Playboys * Larry Wilmore * D. Harlan Wilson * Gahan Wilson * Jackie Wilson * Mehitobel Wilson * Robert Anton Wilson * S. Clay Wilson * Staci Layne Wilson * Amy Winehouse * Alex Winter * Douglas E. Winter * Edgar Winter * Johnny Winter * Robert Wise * Bill Withers * Basil Wolverton * Bobby Womack * Stevie Wonder * Ed Wood, Jr. * Wallace Wood * Jim Woodring * Mary Woronov * Bernie Worrell * Edgar Wright * Steven Wright * William Wyler * XTC * "Weird Al" Yankovich * The Yardbirds * Mercedes M. Yardley * Yeah Yeah Yeahs * Yes * Neil Young * Gary Z * Frank Zappa * Robert Zemeckis * Rob Zombie * The Zombies * John Zorn * Zucker, Abrahams and Zucker * Alan Zweibel * ZZ Top

Appendix B

SCOOB'S LAST WILL AND TESTAMENT

{AUTHOR'S NOTE —What follows is the Facebook post in which I memorialized and said goodbye to the astonishing soul to whom this book is dedicated. No record of this period of my life is complete without it. Everyone who ever met her knows why.]

John Skipp is forever in love with his best friend and best girl Scooby Hamilton, who keeled over and died in a flash this evening, at 7:30 California time (the only time she ever knew, being a California gal). I am in shock, of course. Which leaves me strangely calm. And I hope this serves me well, as I attempt this eulogy.

Can't tell the whole story of her life right now. It's too long and rich and full of incident. But I can tell you that she was one happy camper. A radiant joy bomb, so contagiously excited by the fact of being alive that it wriggled through her every waking gesture (and showed up in her dreams, as well). Half-pit, half-dachshund, insofar as we could tell, she was like a wiener dog on steroids, with this incredibly muscular body and these teeny-tiny legs, that made her like a hilarious cartoon. An incongruous impossibility, in canine flesh.

I met her at a time when I desperately needed love, with the simpler the conditions the better (there is, of course, no unconditional love). And she was totally down for that. Once we figured each other out, it was all smooth sailing. We daily took hour-long walks through the wending hills of Mt. Washington—me respecting her need to investigate every speck of pertinent phenomena, and check her pee-mail; she respecting my need to check mine, and get on with my day—and these moments, taken together, account for a trillion of the greatest moments of my life. Two simple creatures, cheerfully chilling together, enjoying and respecting the shit out of each other.

I could go on and on about her strength and sweetness, her inability to hold her licker (best dog kisses in the world), the sheer joy of hugging and playing with and feeding her, caring for her, honored to have her sleep at the foot of my bed, and being a lucky-ass part of her day-to-day life. I could talk about all the years she added to my life, just by being here. How much it means to me. And will elsewhere. There's just so much to say.

But I want to talk about her death a little, because that's

the thing that just happened.

For the last two weeks, when we took the dirt road that wends above the canyon, she had been desperately tugging toward the precipice. Down where the coyotes live.

And I was like, "SCOOB! JESUS! They'll kill ya!" And every time I said it, I knew that SHE KNEW. That her soul was yanking toward one final tussle. One last manic grapple with her kind. Which she would engage in ferociously, and gleefully. Outnumbered but undaunted. And in the end, expire.

But I wouldn't let her. I wouldn't let her die that way.

So she said, "Okay. I guess I'll just die with you guys who love me."

Which is exactly what she did.

Tonight, at 7:25, my dearest friend Laura Lee Bahr parked her car and walked toward our scheduled meeting. As she was walking, Scoob poked her snoot out through the balcony railing and barked in greeting. Laura barked back. And all our dogs raced toward the front door, as is their custom.

I answered the doorbell as it rang, grabbed Scoob by the collar, and pulled her back as I opened the front door. It's a move that we pulled all the time. I got the door about three inches open. And then she keeled over.

I inched the door a little more. "Scoob! Come on!" I said. Pulled her back a little. Laura tried to get in. And that's when my housemate Frank Blocker said, "She's not breathing."

And I gotta tell ya: Frank did everything he could in those next seconds-turned-to-minutes. Worked her lungs to push out air. Checked her throat for obstructions, of which there were none. Did everything he could, with me beside him.

But she was already floating above us.

Our housemate Max came down from cooking delicious dog dinner, as Laura alerted him. All the other dogs were there. Max picked her up, and together we blasted down the hill to the animal hospital, five minutes away: Max at the wheel, me just holding Scoob in the back seat, and loving her still-warm body just a little more.

But she was gone, and that was that.

So here's what I have to say.

Scoob—by choice or by design—died the best fucking death she could possibly have. Over in a second. Surrounded by loved ones. At the end of a beautiful day. At the end of a beautiful life.

I hope to God I handle my departure that well.

And salute my sweetest sweetheart.

I hope to God we meet again.

— May 31st, 2015

ACKNOWLEDGMENTS

This is the part where I get to thank some people (and one dog in particular) who incited, inspired, put up with, or otherwise helped me survive the crazy decade in which these nice stories were written. (YAAAAY!!! *I love this part!*)

Let's start with the people who originally published 'em: Brad C. Hodson and Benjamin Kane Etheridge, who commissioned me to write "Food Fight" for their awesome upcoming shared-world anthology *Madhouse*; old friend Mark Sieber of the website Horror Drive-In, who requested a film-based horror story and instead got 26 of them, in the form of my "Alphabet Soup"; Rich Chizmar and Brian Freeman of the venerable publisher Cemetery Dance, whose kind requests for new stories resulted in both "Worm Central Tonite!" and "Rose Goes Shopping"; Ken Wood, John Boden, and Tom Bordonaro of the excellent journal *Shock Totem*, who I sneakily fenagled into picking up both "Depresso" and "Worm"; Chris Alexander, who slapped "Art Is the Devil" in the back of the first new issue of the resurrected classic mag *Gorezone*; my dear friend Scott Bradley, whose beautiful idea to do a benefit anthology for MAG (Mine Awareness Group, removing unexploded ordnance from war-torn countries worldwide) resulted in the deeply admirable *Explosions*, for which "In the Waiting Room" was specifically designed; and Cameron Pierce, whose sublimely David Lynch-inspired anthology *In Heaven, Everything Is Fine* coaxed the very-personal "Zygote Notes" from me. THANKS, YOU GUYS!!!

Next we go to a handful of my closest allies and beloved friends-with-brain-ifits: Andrew Kasch, with whom I make the kind of movies I've always dreamed of, every single chance we get; Cody Goodfellow, with whom I often spin the wildest ideas into even wilder words; Rose O'Keefe, Jeff Burk, Cameron Pierce (again), and Carlton Mellick III of Eraserhead Press for welcoming me (and my Fungasm imprint) into the heart of the Bizarro-and-beyondo publishing tribe; and Marc Levinthal and Laura Lee Bahr, two other humble geniuses I collaborate with actively on multiple fronts. I love you all so much it's ridiculous. Thanks for being the core of my creative team, and letting me be at the core of yours.

On the home front, it all comes down to phenomenal housemates-turned-family-for-life Jane Hamilton, Max Cirigliano, Sadie Sue, the late great Scooby Hamilton (to whom this book is dedicated, and whose eulogy is appendixed at the back), and the rotating cast of excellent friends at Cazador Manor, the place that I call home; my beyond-beautiful daughters and spectacular souls, Melanie Rose and Mykel Jean, of whom I could not be more proud;

their gorgeous and ferocious mother, Marianne, who totally saw them through the hardest parts; Griffin and Willow, my astounding can't-believe-they're-my-grandkids, more alive than life itself; Tim Wise, the devout and incredibly proud-making father to said grandkids; Jesse Combs, Mel's ex-wife and eternally cherished family member; Joel Morgan, who gave Mykey the best husband we could ever have asked for; and Cass Paley, who stepped up far above and beyond when I fell down, and has never stopped being there for everyone ever since. Again: there ain't words for how much I love and thank whatever god there is for your presence in my life.

Extra love for my amazing sisters Linda and Reenie, who will probably never read this book, nor should they, cuz it would just freak them out. But who love me nonetheless, because that's the kind of wonderful people they are. And to my dad, Ervin Skipp, who passed away six months after "Zygote Notes" was written: a man I barely knew, but who imprinted me with intelligence and daring, and in his own way tried to make sure we would all be taken care of. And to my mother Shirley, many years gone, who taught me everything I'd ever need to know about love and empathy: as it turns out, the most important things I'd ever learn.

Past that, it's just a long scroll through every fantastic person I've ever worked with (as an author I published, a talent I made films with, a musician I jammed with), along with every amazing spirit who ever inspired me. And the list is just insanely long. (But I give it a whirl in Appendix A, where I force myself to stop right around 1,200. Go on back and take a peek, when you get a chance!)

As for the book itself, I'm forever indebted to Josh

Malerman for his astonishing intro, Matthew Revert for his breathtaking cover art, and (once again) Cameron Pierce for wanting this to happen, and steering it with me into what it's become. Taking a random slice of conversation I spit out and saying, "THAT'S the name of your book." Then putting it into your hands. Again: I cannot possibly love or thank them more.

Wrapping it up, of course, is all of YOU: the people who are actually reading this shit. THANK YOU SO MUCH for—by whatever means necessary—squeezing it into your brain, heart, and soul.

Let us endeavor to make revelatory art forever.

And—insofar as possible—be the least horrible people we could ever hope to be.

Yer pal in the trenches,

Skipp

About the Author

John Skipp is a *New York Times* bestselling author and editor, whose 25 books have sold millions of copies in a dozen languages worlwide. His first anthology, *Book of the Dead*, laid the foundation in 1989 for modern zombie literature. As a filmmaker, Skipp co-directed the award-winning short film *Stay at Home Dad* as well as a segment in the horror anthology film *Tales of Halloween*. His other credits include the novelization of *Fright Night*, the original script of *A Nightmare on Elm Street 5: The Dream Child*, two AVN Awards, and two Bram Stoker Awards. He was also the lead singer in Mumbo's Brain with Chris Poland of Megadeth. Presently, Skipp writes a column, *Nightmare Royale*, for *Fangoria* and is the founder and head editor of Fungasm Press, publishing groundbreaking fiction by authors such as Laura Lee Bahr and Violet LeVoit. From splatterpunk founding father to bizarro elder statesman, Skipp has influenced a generation of horror and counter-culture artists around the world.